Lucy

You're invited to…

Return to Tyler

Where scandals and secrets
are unleashed in a small town
and love is found around every corner.…

The unforgettable stories continue with

Prescription for Seduction
Darlene Scalera
Feb. 2001

Bride of Dreams
Linda Randall Wisdom
March 2001

And don't miss two very special Tyler prequels,
available from Harlequin Historicals

Night Hawk's Bride
Jillian Hart
April 2001

The Nanny
Judith Stacy
May 2001

Dear Reader,

It's February—the month of love. And what better way to celebrate Valentine's Day than with a Harlequin American Romance novel.

This month's selection begins with the latest installment in the RETURN TO TYLER series. *Prescription for Seduction* is what Darlene Scalera offers when sparks fly between a lovely virgin and a steadfast bachelor doctor. *The Bride Said, "Surprise!"* is another of Cathy Gillen Thacker's THE LOCKHARTS OF TEXAS, and is a tender tale about a secret child who brings together two long-ago lovers. (Watch for Cathy's single title, *Texas Vows: A McCabe Family Saga*, next month from Harlequin Books.)

In Millie Criswell's charming new romance, *The Pregnant Ms. Potter* is rescued from a blizzard by a protective rancher who takes her into his home—and into his heart. And in *Longwalker's Child* by Debra Webb, a proud Native American hero is determined to claim the child he never knew existed, but first he has to turn the little girl's beautiful guardian from his sworn enemy into his loving ally.

So this February, treat yourself to all four of our wonderful Harlequin American Romance titles. And in March, look for Judy Christenberry's *Rent a Millionaire Groom*, the first book in Harlequin American Romance's new promotion, 2001 WAYS TO WED.

Wishing you happy reading,

Melissa Jeglinski
Associate Senior Editor
Harlequin American Romance

PRESCRIPTION FOR SEDUCTION
Darlene Scalera

HARLEQUIN®

TORONTO • NEW YORK • LONDON
AMSTERDAM • PARIS • SYDNEY • HAMBURG
STOCKHOLM • ATHENS • TOKYO • MILAN • MADRID
PRAGUE • WARSAW • BUDAPEST • AUCKLAND

Special thanks and acknowledgment are given to Darlene Scalera for her contribution to the RETURN TO TYLER series.

With love to my cousin, Cindy Meyer, whose compassion has become her career and whose shared giggles and excited whispers two days before Christmas are only one of many memories cherished.

ISBN 0-373-16861-6

PRESCRIPTION FOR SEDUCTION

ABOUT THE AUTHOR

Darlene Scalera is a native New Yorker who graduated magna cum laude from Syracuse University with a degree in public communications. She worked in a variety of fields, including telecommunications and public relations, before devoting herself full-time to romance fiction writing. She was instrumental in forming the Saratoga, New York, chapter of Romance Writers of America and is a frequent speaker on romance writing at local schools, libraries, writing groups and women's organizations. She currently lives happily ever after in upstate New York with her husband, Jim, and their two children, J.J. and Ariana. You can write to Darlene at P.O. Box 217, Niverville, NY 12130.

Books by Darlene Scalera

HARLEQUIN AMERICAN ROMANCE

Who's Who in Tyler

Brady Spencer—With all his brothers finally married, only Brady is left to fight off the wily women of Tyler.

Eden Frazier—Can a twenty-seven-year-old maiden who lives with her cat transform herself into a femme fatale?

Caroline Benning—No one knows much about the new waitress at Marge's Diner.

Cooper Night Hawk—The deputy keeps his eye on all newcomers, especially the suspicious Ms. Benning.

Wayne Donovan—The hunky express deliveryman would love to put his relationship with Eden on the fast track.

Gina Eber—She's always on the trail of a juicy story to sizzle the pages of the *Tyler Citizen*.

Nadine—The Hair Affair's new stylist knows a lot about hairdos and even more about men.

Annabelle Scanlon—The postmistress dishes out the mail—and the latest scandal.

Chapter One

Brady Spencer came to Eden only at night. When the phone was quiet, the front door locked, the last customer gone hours ago. Only the light inside the display refrigerator remained bright. The garden scents seemed stronger.

Eden studied the table before her scattered with foam, floral tape, chicken wire, ribbon, flowers. She picked up a yielding lily and when she saw her hand was trembling, she closed her eyes, feeling foolish. There was a light knock at the back door. He always used the back door. She heard the handle turning, the door opening. The door was left unlocked. Eden opened her eyes, stayed her hands against the cool Formica tabletop.

Even before he opened the door, Brady smelled the sweetness. A sweetness different from blood's hot smell or the operating room's white, close scent. He stepped inside, closed the door, took a breath. Heaven would smell like this.

"Eden?" His voice was low, but still heard in the surrounding quiet.

"Doctor." She appeared in the back room's archway. In her hand she held a thin-stemmed flower, its large petals furled back, unafraid to reveal its secrets.

"Come in." The flower pointed the way. "I'm just finishing an arrangement for the front windows."

Brady smiled. Eden's lush window displays were legendary. Tomorrow passersby would stop and stare like children in front of a pastry shop.

He followed her. The dark apron that covered her had been left undone in the back, its ties hanging loosely. The shift she wore beneath it was shapeless, a long column moving down her body, unbroken except for the push of small, rounded hips. The apron's ties swung, and he saw her body's curves come, change with a single sway, then disappear beneath the pale print. He looked up, realizing the feminine form he'd been ogling was Eden. His interest became unease. He looked away only to see more color, shape, proportion in the tubs, watering cans and jugs of flowers and greens. Spring had just begun in southern Wisconsin, but here, it reigned endless. He breathed in, gathering the composure that had made him one of the most trusted surgeons at Tyler General.

Eden had seen the frown appear on Brady's face as he'd looked away. She dropped her gaze to the flowers on the table, envying them their beauty. "So another order?'' She broke the silence. ''Who's the unsuspecting recipient this time?''

He looked at her. Her face was without makeup, her dark-brown hair pulled tight into a ponytail that stressed the shapes of her features—broad, almost flat cheeks, a colorless mouth. It was an ordinary face on an ordinary woman. She was average in height, only she seemed smaller, swallowed by the apron hanging loose, the formless dress that stretched to the jut of her thin ankles. There mint-green socks wrinkled above dull black loafers, the kind with the wide fit and the puckered seams worn by many of his elderly female patients.

His gaze moved to her hands, pale against the perfection of the flowers. Her wrists were thin. There was a vulnerability about her that made her appear much younger than her years. There was a quiet to her that made her seem much older. Both discouraged ogling. Still he had an urge to kneel and pull up those socks until they climbed smooth up her calves, ending just below her knees that had to be endearingly knobby. His unease crept in again.

She concentrated on the table before her, her shoulders hunched, her head bowed as if she were listening to the flowers. She taped leafy greens to a thin, pointed stick, angled it in among the others, adjusted a slender yellow-and-white bloom. She lifted her gaze back to him. He saw those eyes— large, round and made even more remarkable when compared to the surrounding ordinary features. These eyes didn't just see, they fascinated, they divined, they reminded one that miracles did exist—all through an undefinable color. Its base was purple, but darker than the frail shade of an iris, lighter than the red-purple of a grape. It wasn't the purplish-blue of periwinkle or the pale shadow of lilac nor the strong purple prized by royalty. It was a shade that belonged only to Eden.

She smiled, the shape of her face gentling. "Or has the Flower Phantom decided to reveal his identity?"

The Flower Phantom. The name had been coined in Gina Eber's column in the *Tyler Citizen* about the recent secret flower deliveries around town. There'd been other anonymous gifts—the motorized toy jeeps to take the children cancer patients to chemotherapy; the DVD players with a complete collection of Jerry Lewis films for long-term care. But it was the flowers everyone remembered the most.

Eden unrolled some wire and clipped it. "Gina's a good friend of mine, you know. In fact, she's been stopping by the shop even more frequently." She met Brady's gaze.

"You don't think she knows, do you?"

"She brought up the subject once or twice." Eden looped a length of ribbon back and forth. "I told her that was privileged information between a florist and her client."

He heard the unexpected jest in her soft voice. He remembered the push of her hips as she walked, the hint of curves and rounds. He couldn't look away.

For a moment neither did she. When she finally

did, he followed her gaze to the flowers waiting for her. There he saw blooms of purple. He searched for the shade of her eyes. He was a man who liked things defined.

"What color are your eyes?"

Her cheeks flushed, the deep-red seeming to alter her eye color. He hadn't meant to make her uncomfortable by blurting out the question.

"People tell me it's violet." She looked down again, busying herself with the flowers. Only her blush was left exposed.

"Violet." To most, it was a color. But he knew it as a woman's name, a name he'd been forbidden to say since the age of eleven.

"Violet." He said it again defiantly. Once there would've been no response inside him. Lately that hadn't been the case.

He focused on the silent girl in front of him. Seeing the blush still on her cheeks, he chose his words carefully. "Your eyes...they're unusual."

She raised her head, not sure if she'd been complimented or diagnosed. She knew she wasn't beautiful. Beautiful would have been divine. Nor was she ugly. Ugly would have been, at least, interesting. She was plain. Bland as unbuttered macaroni. Except for her eyes. But they were so at odds with the rest of her physical appearance that instead of rescuing her, they only served to confirm that even the gods sometimes made mistakes.

She knew all this before Brady fixed his gaze on her and offered a compliment in the same tone he might use to note the discovery of a rare disease. She also knew how ridiculous she was, imagining his presence here was for any reason other than that she had the most beautiful flowers in Tyler and several miles beyond.

"So what kind of an arrangement would you like to send?" Eden moved the conversation back to business, where it belonged.

He looked at the buckets of eucalyptus and narcissus, the stiff stalks of delphiniums, the clusters of daffodils curving beneath the weight of closed buds. "I want something exotic." He waved the hands that healed. "Something exciting."

She didn't realize she'd sighed aloud until he glanced at her. She covered with a bright smile and a light voice that teased, "Don't we all?"

His expression went from curious to uncertain. "I suppose." He moved to inspect the aluminum shelves of vases and foam-filled containers lining the far wall.

His back was to her, yet she didn't turn to take him in. She didn't have to. She knew without sight his back's strong width, his shoulders' proud slope, the faint pink where the barber had shaved the nape of his neck. She'd had a crush on him since she was eight. She'd been crossing to the park and tripped on the curb. Instead of laughing at her like the other older boys hanging out in the square had done, he'd come and helped her up, asked her if she was all right, his face serious and already adult as he examined her knees. From that moment her heart had been his, even though her head knew her fantasies were futile.

Then he had come into her flower shop late one night over a month ago.

She heard him move. The temptation became too great, and she turned and looked at him. She'd been born without beauty, but every day she created it, surrounded herself with it, gave it to others. Most of all she knew when it was before her.

It was before her now. She looked at him and, for a moment, was adrift.

She looked away before he caught her. As well as she knew beauty, she also knew what she created often fell short of reality, what she craved could never be completely hers.

He asked about a vase. She walked to where he stood.

"This one?" She took the vase off the shelf, its weight cool against her palms. "It has lovely lines, don't you think? And the size, the balance of the body is certainly strong enough to hold its own with the most exotic mixtures."

He touched the vase in her hands and nodded approval.

"I hope these exciting flowers aren't for a patient with a heart condition or high blood pressure." She kept the conversation friendly. They were, after all, friends. It would have to be enough.

He smiled. She was pleased. He didn't smile enough. His brows often pulled low as if weighted with worry. Two deep lines angled above his nose, creating a constant stern impression. Some nights, though, she would make small jokes and small talk, and the lines on his face would smooth.

"Actually, these flowers aren't for a patient at all."

"No?" She walked to the design table, the vase heavy in her hands. A woman? Why not? Brady and his brothers had inspired more female fantasies within the town limits of Tyler than George Clooney and a case of Asti Spumante combined. But the two other brothers had both married within the past four months, leaving only one single Spencer brother—Brady—to fight off the wily women of Tyler. Eden had no doubt Brady's bachelor days were numbered.

"The flowers are for a nurse."

Of course.

"Cece Baron."

"Cece Baron?" Eden's quiet voice went an octave higher.

He glanced at her curiously. "You know, Jeff's wife."

Eden did know. Cece was the nursing supervisor at Worthington House, and together with Jeff, Tyler General's chief of staff, had seven-year-old twin girls.

"Don't you think your boss is going to have something to say if his wife starts receiving bouquets of flowers from a secret admirer?"

"I hope so."

She frowned. "You're sure about this?"

"Definitely, after I saw Cece sitting in Jeff's office today, waiting for him. She was looking at a family picture Jeff has in his office—I think it was taken at his younger sister Liza's wedding. Cece was crying.''

Eden's frown deepened.

''She put on a big smile when she saw me, but she knew I'd seen her. She'd said she was being silly. That between her work and Jeff's schedule and the twins, she couldn't expect things to be like they once were between her and her husband.''

''Like they once were?''

''Crazy, wild in love, passionate, head-over-heels, you know.'' Brady spoke with a doctor's detachment.

Eden didn't know, but she nodded, anyway.

''Cece finally told me Jeff and she had made a lunch date, just the two of them. Some 'together' time to try and put a little magic back in the marriage. She'd waited forty-five minutes before she'd found out he'd left the hospital an hour ago to take some prospective donors to lunch to discuss building a new imaging facility. He'd forgotten about their date. 'Imagine,' she'd said. 'Stood up by your own husband. How humiliating is that?' But she made me promise not to tell him she was there. Said it'd only upset him, and she was already worried enough about his stress level.''

Eden's features relaxed. ''But she didn't make you promise not to send an anonymous arrangement of flowers that she might assume was an apology from her husband?''

Brady smiled. "Let's send one to Jeff, too. Maybe that'll put a little mystique back into the marriage." She heard an uncustomary excitement in his voice. He looked away, and if Eden didn't know better, she would've sworn Tyler General's most unflappable surgeon was suddenly self-conscious.

"It's a lovely thought," she assured him, hoping to ease his discomfort.

"Unsigned, of course." His voice was even once again. He returned his gaze to her.

"Of course." She wondered if he'd ever believe that his vulnerability didn't make him weak, merely human.

"If the chief of staff knew one of his surgeons was playing Cupid, well, you can imagine how that would go over at the monthly staff meetings."

"Of course." She always agreed. It was part of the ritual. He walked around the shop, his briefcase gripped in his right hand and his steps brisk. His left hand tapped the curved sales counter, made a wrought-iron birdcage sway, asserted control over his surroundings.

"What about these?" He tapped on the cooler's door, his nose inches from the glass. "These white things in the corner. What are they?"

"Calla lilies. Special order received today. They're lovely, don't you think?"

"They look exotic enough."

"Oh, they are. Add nothing more than some camellia leaves or laurel, and you've got yourself a beautiful bouquet." She studied the oversize blooms. "They'd also be stunning mixed with white French tulips and paperwhites."

Brady nodded as if he knew what she was talking about. They both knew he had no idea.

"Put a big bow around the vase," he said. It was a voice that suffered no fools, especially himself. He had a reputation as one of the best doctors around and also one of the most demanding. Eden suspected, however, he was hardest on himself.

"Always a big bow."

"Good." He smiled, satisfied.

Now that wasn't so painful, was it? she thought as if she were the doctor and he, the patient.

"Charge it to my card as usual." Business done, he turned to go. He was a busy man. Too busy, Eden thought. The first night he'd lingered, asking irrelevant questions as if needing to talk. One night she might coax him to again stay longer, sit with her, have a cup of tea, but not tonight. Tonight she wasn't brave enough, and he wasn't calm enough.

"Eden?" He'd turned, catching her studying him.

"Yes?" She dropped her gaze to the table, pretending to inspect the arrangement.

"Thank you."

She looked at him.

"You're..." He cleared his throat. "You're swell." He turned, went through the arch and was gone.

Swell? Eden stared at the doorway. She looked back at the splay of flowers before her on the table. She twisted a peony to the left for balance.

"Swell?" She spoke to the flowers. The peony's heavy head bobbed as if confirming.

She circled the arrangement, her practiced eye checking the line, color, rhythm.

"Is that what he told that sleek blonde he had dinner with at the Old Heigelburg a few weeks ago? And what about that big-chested, big-haired brunette spoon-feeding him Marge's apple pie not two days later at the diner? I suppose she was *swell*, too?"

The flowers were silent as if knowing the answer as well as she did. With Brady's movie-star looks, commanding presence and dark charm, it was no secret that the patients of Tyler General weren't the only ones who sought out the doctor's renowned skills. His success with single women was as well-known as his acclaimed professional reputation.

Yet Eden knew she was the only one with whom Brady had shared the secret of his anonymous good deeds. The thought made her smile. It also made her feel special. Not beautiful or exciting like the flowers he chose or the many women he dated. But she felt privileged to share a side of Brady Spencer that no one else knew or even suspected. No, it wasn't love or passion, a far cry from that, but still it was something.

She misted the flowers and carried them to a draped pedestal in the front window. "Don't worry, Dr. Spencer." The room was quiet except for the hum of the lights and the gurgle of the fish tank. "Your secrets are safe with me."

SWELL? Brady walked down the thin alley between the flower shop and the beauty salon. He was a highly trained, skilled surgeon. Why was he talking like some jug-eared kid with a cowlick? He reached the street and turned toward the condominium complex where he lived.

It was Eden, he decided. Eden with her innocence, her guileless smile, her wonderful world so removed from the reality he knew. He stepped into The Garden, and he was eleven again—insecure, confused, wanting—all beneath a facade of bravado and bluster.

He stopped to cross at the corner, already recognizing the restlessness that would have him prowling around his efficient, empty condo until early-morning hours. His apartment was close to the hospital, and he often walked the short distance no matter the weather. In fact, battling the winter cold and winds gave him as much satisfaction as strolling in the sun. This year, though, spring had come unusually early. The record-warm March had melted the snows and muddied the ground and brought out others not so brave or belligerent to walk the icy streets like Brady.

There was no traffic but he hadn't crossed. He sighed, turning almost automatically toward the hospital and the piles of paperwork that might quell his unrest. He saw Martha Bauer on the arm of her daughter, Anna Kelsey, coming up the street. Even from a block away, Martha's blue eyes pinned him.

He strode toward the women, seeing no reason

for concern. If they'd seen him coming out of the alley next to The Garden of Eden, they'd probably assume he'd taken a shortcut home from the hospital.

"Good evening, ladies." He greeted them a half block away, his smile sociable but his steps smart.

"You're turning in the wind like a weathervane, Doc."

Martha's eyes held him fast, slowed his step. "I've never known you to lose your way." The old woman's smile was as sharp as her gaze. "Or to admit it, at least."

Martha's daughter, Anna, looked apologetically at Brady, her eyes the same blue as her mother's, only softer. "Now Dr. Spencer knows why all his other patients at Worthington House have high blood pressure."

Brady continued to smile pleasantly, professionally. "I'm not lost," he assured Martha. "Just on my way back to the hospital to catch up on some paperwork."

Martha studied him. "You always were the most serious son."

"I thought I was the most charming one," Brady deadpanned.

The older woman folded her arms across her chest. "When are you going to settle down and get married like your brothers?"

"Mom!" Anna shook her head, the evening light blending the gray in her dark hair.

"What? No more single Spencer men in Tyler?"

Brady smiled. "The place would become a ghost town."

"No more single Spencer men in Tyler?" A glint had appeared in Martha's blue eyes. "Are you telling me something I don't know about your father and Lydia Perry?"

Brady eyed the elderly woman. "Is there something I should know about my father and Lydia? The Quilting Circle hasn't started a new quilt, have they?"

Martha studied him as if trying to determine if he was teasing or serious.

"Brady, did Quinn and Molly tell you how much my grandson, Jeremy, adores Sara?" Anna diplomatically changed the subject. "They're inseparable at Kaity's Kids."

Brady's smile widened at the mention of his brother's new wife and her daughter. "I agree with Jeremy one hundred percent. Sara is a charming child. Pure adorable."

"And it won't be long before Seth and Jenna will be bringing new little ones to the Spencer Sunday dinners, will it?"

Brady nodded. "Jenna is due in May."

"Imagine, twins." Anna shook her head again.

"Humph," Martha sounded. "Elias will never be the same."

Brady had to agree. Everything was changing. After many years, the somber Spencer family home stretching along Maple Street was again hearing the sound of children's laughter, the song of women's voices.

Martha's gaze remained on Brady. "So, why aren't you dating anyone, Doc?"

"I'm dating, Martha. As much and as many as I can."

The old lady smiled slyly. "Spring is in the air, Brady Spencer." She gestured toward the flowers displayed in The Garden of Eden's front windows. "Good time to stop and smell the roses."

He looked at the flowers in the soft light, thought of Eden's thin, white hands arranging them until they were even more perfect. Past the shop windows it was dark except for the fish tank's purplish glow and the low light from the cooler. Eden must've gone up to her apartment over the store for the night.

"Eden's a good girl, isn't she?" Martha asked. He stepped back from the window, but it was too late. His study of the store hadn't gone unnoticed by the old woman.

He carefully composed his reply. "She seems like a nice person."

Martha's eyes narrowed. "You know her, don't you?"

"Sure, everybody knows Eden."

Martha tilted her head back, her gaze gaining new power. "She could be easy to overlook. She's not flashy and noisy like some I've seen. She's the kind of girl that lets a man hear the sound of his own breath."

"Mom," Anna interrupted, "we're keeping the

good doctor from his work.'' She again smiled apologetically at Brady.

Martha's gaze never left Brady. "I think I'll keep an eye on you, Doc."

Brady knew the elderly woman's sharp tongue protected a soft heart. He knew because it was a tactic he himself had mastered. "If somebody's got to, Martha, I'm glad it's you." He leaned over and kissed the woman's cheek, felt the precarious thinness of flesh.

He stepped back, concealing his own surprise at his behavior. Martha touched her cheek, but snorted with indignation. "It should be someone with a lot fewer years and a lot more agreeable. Someone like—"

"C'mon, Mom." Anna hooked her arm through her mother's. "If we don't get you back by bingo, the home will be calling in Deputy Cooper. Nice seeing you, Brady."

"You too, Anna. Tell Johnny I said hello."

"Can I tell him you said he should go easy on those onion rings when the Dairy King opens for the season next month?"

With relief, Brady returned to his professional role. "With his hiatal hernia, the chili dogs, too."

Anna glanced at Martha. "And maybe egg substitutes and a little less bacon for Mom at those Sunday breakfasts at the diner? Her last blood workup showed her cholesterol was high."

"Couldn't hurt." He looked at Martha. "No sense courting heart disease."

"If you're in such a big hurry to get me home, why are we still standing around here flapping our jaws?" Martha snapped at her daughter.

"No wonder he's not settled down yet," the old woman was still grumbling as she and Anna crossed to the square. "He's too busy making sure the good citizens of Tyler live long, unhappy lives."

Brady watched the women walk away. Even after they disappeared behind the oak trees, he stood, trying to figure out what had prompted his sudden show of affection. He wasn't one given to spontaneous gestures...until lately. He shook his head. At times he didn't understand himself anymore.

He looked up. The windows above the flower shop were covered with lace, the light past them tinted pearl-pink. He took a deep breath, swore he smelled heaven once more before he started toward the hospital.

The security guard glanced up as the double glass doors to the hospital's main lobby slid open. The regular entrance to the brick annex where most of the doctors had their offices was locked after hours to save on security costs. The guard nodded at Brady. "Thought your day was done, Doc."

Brady only had to say one word. "Paperwork."

The guard nodded again. "The modern man's burden."

"You have a good evening now." Brady headed down the corridor. His encounter with Martha had scared him off small talk for the night.

The hall was windowless, lit by fluorescent tubes

in the ceiling that made shadows seem to disappear and turned faces hard. He said hello as he passed a cleaning lady. The floor was bland asphalt tiles. The walls were a faded mauve.

He turned into another, shorter hall that led to a tunnel connecting the smaller professional center to the hospital. At the tunnel's end, he took the stairs to the second floor. He inserted his key card into the door and went into the empty waiting room. He passed reception, the records room, examining rooms, the offices of the other doctors in the practice before coming to his own. He unlocked the door, seeing the charts piled on top of the corner file cabinet. Several white lab jackets on wire hangers hung from the coatrack next to the cabinet. The blinds were drawn. Beneath the room's only window was a sofa he'd never rested on.

He set down his briefcase and grabbed a handful of charts. Sitting at his desk, he took a microcassette recorder and some pens and pencils out of the top drawer.

He looked at the charts before him and heaved a deep breath. Heaven was gone. Here, even behind the office's closed door, he could only smell the bitter scent of sickness, the false lemon of antiseptic.

He'd thought he would get used to it. He never had. Each time, whether in his office or the operating room, it was still a shock—the compressed smells, the soundless slice into skin, the easy break of bone. It scared the hell out of him. But what had scared him the most was his own fear—the feeling of being vulnerable, not in control. And so, he'd had no choice but to specialize in surgery.

He opened a chart but didn't look at it. The walls of his office were the same nonthreatening color as throughout the hospital. The lighting was surreal. The linens in the exam rooms and everywhere else were an innocuous white. The beds were metal. The gowns were thin and fashioned to expose.

He thought of the flower shop with its color, its life, and suddenly he longed for its quiet. It wasn't the eerie quiet of the hospital but a calm, content silence. A quiet one would imagine to be in the paradise The Garden was named after.

He'd gone there on a whim. That had been the beginning, the first spontaneous act in an otherwise orderly life. It had been the soulless month of February. He'd been walking home, tired, frustrated, wondering if there was a world where there were no Februarys. He'd been thinking of a patient, a woman all alone, old, frail, arthritis ballooning her fingers, curving them at odd angles so that even holding a cup became a feat.

She'd come in with a hip fracture and her whole life in a worn black leather pocketbook. Her history showed several ministrokes. She'd be transferred to a nursing home as soon as a bed opened up. All day, through rounds, meetings, consultations, Brady had thought of that woman, sitting alone in her thin-mattressed bed, staring, her mauve walls bare as she moved more toward death than life. They'd done all they could for her medically. Still he'd wanted to do more. Some would say he did enough every day with his prescriptions and sutures and killer smile. For him, it wasn't enough any longer.

That evening he'd walked the few blocks from the hospital to home, passing The Garden of Eden. In the front windows there'd been flowers from winter-whites and palest pastels to summer brights and heady deep tones the color of ecstasy. He'd stopped. He wasn't sure why. Maybe it was the lipstick-red so startling at the ends of the tulips' yellow petals. Maybe it was the spray of baby's breath like the first snow. Maybe it was nothing more than to stand somewhere and see only color and life. He had no reason, but he went to the door. Just to look around inside a few minutes, he had told himself as he'd turned the knob. It had been locked, but as he turned to go, the door had opened. Eden had seen him at the windows and had unlocked the door. Finally he was inside, his steps too quick, the charcoal-gray of his suit too drab. Yet the scents lured him, kept him long. And there'd been Eden with her own soft style and extraordinary eyes. She had said a few words in her quiet way, then leaned toward him as if only wanting to listen. And he, who never revealed, had told her about the elderly patient alone in the empty, faded room. By the time he'd left, he'd ordered an extravagant arrangement to be sent anonymously to the woman. He'd also felt better than he could ever remember.

The next day he'd stopped by the shop again after hours and had another lavish bouquet sent to the woman, then another and another, filling her room with flowers until even the other patients, visitors and nurses stopped as they passed and sighed with pleasure.

The woman had died at the end of the week— pneumonia complications—but Brady knew she had died surrounded by life and color and beauty and the thought that somebody cared. She hadn't died like his mother, her smile not being seen again by those who needed to see it most.

Now Brady sent flowers almost every other day. There was always someone alone or sick or with a heavy heart. The deliveries were never signed. The flowers were always ordered after hours. Brady wouldn't jeopardize his patients' confidence or the hospital staff's respect by being anything other than the strong, sensible, self-sufficient surgeon they expected. He had learned at the age of eleven never to expose your weaknesses. And he never had...until he'd gone to Eden.

Chapter Two

Cookies. Brady smelled cookies. Mixed in with the rose and the lavender, the sandalwood and the gardenia, there was cinnamon, melting sugar and a richness so dense, the air around him seemed thick.

"Eden," he called, his voice sounding slow and full in the fat air.

"Hello, Brady."

He looked to the right, past the deep stainless steel sink and the crowded shelves to the stairs that led to the second floor. On the landing two big fuzzy bumblebees, their antennae bobbing, greeted him. From the whimsical slippers, Eden's thin, bare legs stretched up like lollipop sticks into baggy shorts beneath an oversize cotton shirt. Her hair was pulled back, twisted up high and tight into a knot, except for two ends that had broken free. They stuck up like the rabbit ears children sneak behind another's head in a photo. She came down the stairs fast and, at the bottom, paused, panting. She smiled, a faint pink in her cheeks and her eyes the deep purple of dawn. He wanted to kiss her so badly, he could almost taste her like the promise of cookies that came down the stairwell. He wanted to take her right there on the softly lit stairs with the swirl of smells around them.

Great. He'd gone from leering at Eden to seeing her stretched out, waiting for him on the staircase. Guilt grabbed him, gave him a hard shake. Shame came next. This was Eden—sweet, awkward Eden who taught the ladies auxiliary how to make balsam wreaths for the Christmas bazaar and made sure Guy Teator, the oldest resident of Worthington House but still the snappiest dresser in Tyler, always had a fresh boutonniere, free of charge.

She was in no way the type of woman that normally drew his attention. He preferred a more sophisticated type of woman. A woman with more curves, with artfully curled hair and carefully chosen clothes. A worldly, ambitious woman who enjoyed a relationship based on mutual respect and physical pleasures. A woman who didn't expect a long-term commitment.

Eden wasn't that type of woman.

He saw her spindly legs, her knees as he'd imagined, hard and round as apples picked too early. No, Eden was the opposite of the woman he usually dated.

Eden was the type of girl who'd fall in love.

He was staring again. Eden looked at her oversize bee slippers. Could she blame him? Had she really imagined desire in those jade green eyes? This had to stop. *She* had to stop.

Yet she said, "I baked cookies."

"I shouldn't have come." He spoke in the tone of a man who was listened to, but he was leaning on the edge of the sink where the flowers were processed. "It's too late. I've kept you up."

"They're oatmeal chocolate butterscotch." A buzzer sounded from the second floor. "Oops, there's the timer." She turned and trotted up the steps. Brady hesitated, then followed those fuzzy yellow feet up the stairs.

The door at the top opened into a blue and white kitchen. Cookies cooled on the counter, the heat and smells welcoming him as if he'd come home.

Eden switched off the timer and opened the oven door. More heat and smells came like a child's hungry dream, and, at that moment, Brady couldn't think of anything more wonderful than warm oatmeal chocolate butterscotch cookies.

Eden straightened, the cookie sheet in her gloved hand, her face flushed, her eyes bright from the heat. He'd seen a similar look on women before, but they hadn't been baking. They'd been in his bed.

He looked away. He was irredeemable. There was only one thing that could save him, that had always saved him. He looked at Eden. "Can I help you?" he asked.

"Yes."

He was saved.

"You can sit down and eat as many of these

cookies as possible before I do.'' She blew at a strand of hair that had fallen across her forehead and smiled at him.

He saw the rows of cookies cooling on the wire racks. Since lunch he'd only had three large cups of black coffee and a cranberry juice grabbed off a nutrition cart on its way to the floors. He took off his suit jacket, hung it evenly across the kitchen chair's high back. ''I could do that.''

She set a ceramic plate piled with cookies in the center of the round table and a smaller matching plate before him. ''Something to drink?''

He leaned back, a content man. Her hand, covered with the oversize pot holder, jerked away from the back of his chair where it'd been resting. He glanced up at her.

She looked at him with her dark-violet eyes and her delicate smile. Her hand covered with the plaid pot holder was now gripping the other, bare one.

''Tea?'' she offered, taking another step back.

He hated tea. ''Tea would be great.'' He pushed back his chair. ''But let me help you.''

''No, no.'' Her hands flew apart and patted the air above his shoulders. ''You sit.''

She moved about the kitchen, filling the bright-red teakettle and setting it back on the stove, opening the stenciled cupboard, standing on her tiptoes and reaching up to the tea boxes on the upper shelf.

''Let's see, I've got orange pekoe, cinnamon apple, peppermint...'' She looked over her shoulder at him.

"Whatever you prefer."

Her gaze moved to his empty plate, then back to him. "Eat, Brady." Her voice was low and coaxing; her smile quiet. She waited until he reached for the cookie plate before turning back to the tea boxes.

"Mmm, orange pekoe, I think." She opened another cupboard, took out two brightly colored mugs, shook a tea bag into each. On the stove, the kettle steamed.

Brady looked around the tiny kitchen as full of colors and patterns and shapes as the store below. Hand-painted plates hung on one wall. A vine was about to flower on the scalloped shelf above the sink. More flowers twined on a grapevine arched above the door and poked from the terra-cotta pots scattered around the room. Home Sweet Home was stenciled on the dish towels that hung from the oven door handle. Through the doorway that led into the next room, he saw peach-colored walls and a framed Norman Rockwell print. Eden was humming. She set a ceramic cow milk pitcher and a matching sugar bowl on the table. Next to them she placed a plastic bear of honey.

"Or do you prefer lemon?" she asked.

Definitely the marrying type. He shook his head. The uneaten cookie still waited in his hand.

A fat tangle of fur sauntered in from the next room.

"There you are, Penelope." Eden set a steaming mug smelling of orange and cloves in front of Brady. "Come and say hello to Dr. Spencer."

The cat stopped in the doorway and stared at Brady, as if reading his every thought.

"So…" Eden sat at the table, her mug cupped in her hands. "You had a late emergency?"

He nodded. The cat stared at him, its pupils narrow. The cookie was going cold in his hand. He took a bite and was ruined forever for any baked goods that came cellophane wrapped.

He finished the cookie in two bites and reached for more. He saw Eden watching him. "These are great."

"Thank you." She dropped her gaze, blew across the tea's surface, but Brady could see she was smiling. She glanced up. The tiny smile was still there. "Have some more."

Brady chewed. *Definitely the marrying type.* He glanced at the cat eyeing him. The cookies stuck in his throat. He picked up the mug beside his plate and took a large sip. He hated tea.

Eden lifted her own mug and sipped. "Good, huh?"

He swished the liquid in his mouth and gulped it down. "Delicious."

Her smile widened, the corners of her eyes lifting. The steam from the cup warmed her face, made her eyes gleam. She had flawless skin, smooth as cream, meant to be touched.

He took a big bite of cookie and focused on the flavors blending in his mouth. He refused to look at Penelope.

"Was it very serious?" Eden asked. "The emergency?"

"Appendectomy. Routine procedure," he said through a mouthful of cookie, "but the patient had been taking aspirin all day for the abdomen pain, and his blood was thinned out. Gave us some trouble clotting, but we got it under control. It just took a while longer."

He took a bite of cookie and chewed. "You know..." He pointed the cookie at her. "You could take over the world with these cookies."

She tipped her head back and laughed. She didn't often laugh so loud and full. Not that she was grim. Not at all. It was just that silent smiles were more her style. This was nice, Brady decided, sitting here in this cozy kitchen, eating homemade cookies, listening to the sweet sound of Eden's laughter.

"I mean it," he said. "One bite would make the mightiest, meanest men your slaves."

Her laughter continued. He watched it ripple up her throat's long length, thinking how white and tender the skin was there.

His thoughts were interrupted by a soft, warm weight landing in his lap. "What the—?"

"Penelope, where's your manners?" Eden scolded. "Get down off Dr. Spencer this minute."

Staring up at Brady, Penelope blinked her wide-set eyes once and plopped dead center in his lap.

"Penelope Maybelle Patterson." Eden sprang up, clapping her hands as she rounded the table. Penelope gave Brady one final slitted look, then slid off his lap.

"Shame on you. Getting cat hair all over Brady's expensive suit." Eden swiped at Brady's pant legs.

One brush of her hands across the length of his thighs and he felt the low, beginning heat of desire. He looked at her. Penelope stared at her, too.

Realizing the intimacy of her touch, Eden stopped. Her face colored. As she straightened, she met Brady's stare and froze, her color deepening.

He smiled the smile used to reassure anxious patients. "You surprise me, Eden."

"I do?" It was a whisper, her vivid-colored eyes wide.

"Do you give all your pets full names?"

A smile started. "Don't you?" She went back to her seat. A little more of her smile returned, but when she picked up her tea, she had to grip the mug with both hands.

"Except for the occasional frog or lightning bug, I never had any pets."

"None?"

"Seth had a collie once when we were young, but it got loose and ran away. About a week later my dad was driving us to the fishing derby up at Timber Lake, and we saw the collie lying on the side of the road. A car had hit him." His gaze moved past her. "We never had any more pets after that."

He picked up his mug and took a sip. He really hated tea.

"I didn't have any brothers or sisters." Eden was

still holding her mug too tightly. "For my parents, after twenty-two years of trying to have children without success, I was a total surprise. A nice one, they always assured me, but after all that time when it'd only been the two of them, I definitely disrupted their lives. Anyway, I guess I always thought of my pets as real people, the brothers and sisters I'd never had."

Brady thought of his own brothers, how close they'd always been—especially after their mother had left them. Not that they ever talked about what happened. Their father had forbidden it. There'd been twenty-three years of silence until a few months ago when his father had relented and given Cooper Night Hawk permission to look into his wife's whereabouts. It was Coop who had found out Violet had died in childbirth seven months after she ran off with another man.

Brady looked into Eden's eyes and cleared his throat. "I guess I should order the flowers I want to send."

She straightened the platter of cookies, pushing it closer to him. "There's plenty of time. Have another cookie."

He picked up a fifth cookie.

"Let me get you a fresh cup of tea." She reached across the table for his mug. "Maybe cinnamon apple this time?"

He saw the concern in her extraordinary eyes. "That'd be great." The words were out of his mouth before he could stop them, his behavior once more surprising him. It wasn't an unpleasant surprise though. He didn't even want to analyze it. He only wanted to watch Eden as she moved around the kitchen. Her face was still tinged with pink, and soon she was humming again. Not an unpleasant surprise at all.

She turned on the burner under the kettle and came back to the table. She looked at him, her hands grasping the edge of her chair. "We'll sit and drink some tea, eat some cookies, and you can tell me all about your day."

WHICH WAS PRECISELY what he did, Brady thought as he walked to the hospital the next morning. It had been almost midnight by the time he'd left Eden's and returned to his condo. He'd slept like a drunken man. Too much sugar, he'd decided.

He sidestepped a puddle. The temperatures had stayed defiantly warm, reducing winter to no more than black patches of soggy soil or an occasional wet stain on the sidewalk. The birds had come home. Women once again wore skirts and short-sleeved shirts baring long stretches of skin. The men walked slower, steadier. Even Brady's steps this morning weren't the usual military march but almost approached a stroll. He'd decided to take the long way around the town square. When he spied Cooper coming out of Marge's Diner, a scowl on his face, it didn't seem possible anyone could be unhappy on this sun-warmed morning.

"Coop."

The town deputy turned, his natural Native American looks made even more dramatic by his brooding expression. He was considered a fourth son to the Spencer family not because of his physical looks but because of the strong emotional bonds between him and the Spencer men. Seeing Brady, he smiled. Still his dark-brown eyes were somber.

Brady smiled at his family's best friend. "Kinda early to look so mean. What happened? Did Marge run out of blueberry pancakes before you got there?"

"Now you know that has never happened in the history of Tyler. And probably never will, God willing." Coop's guarded gaze assessed the doctor. "You seem awful happy for a man whose boss is watching him right now, probably wondering why you're wasting time harassing Tyler's finest when you should be at work."

Through the diner's front windows, Brady saw Jeff Baron seated in one of the red vinyl booths lining the walls. Beside him was Cece. They were both smiling as they waved. Brady waved back, his own grin widening. He was about to turn back to Coop when he noticed the new waitress, Caroline Benning, staring at him from behind the counter. They'd formally met at the Christmas Eve party up at the Timberlake Lodge. He raised his hand to wave hello, but she looked away and began refilling the coffee cups of the diners that occupied every seat at the L-shaped counter.

"That new girl—"

"Caroline Benning." Coop stopped smiling.

"She seems like a nice kid." The two men started walking toward the center of town.

"She's hiding something."

Brady stopped, looked curiously at Coop.

"I can't prove anything yet. It's a feeling I've got. That woman has secrets."

"We all have secrets, Coop." Brady tried to restore his friend's earlier smile.

"Maybe, but that lady has a big secret. I can feel it in my gut."

Brady's surprise increased. Everyone knew Coop was a man who believed in facts, not intuition or other intangible feelings.

"Don't tell me you're listening to all that gossip still going round?"

"I'm not the one who was found tangled up in the shrubs outside your dad's house," Coop pointed out as the two men passed the law firm where Brady's brother, Quinn, was a partner.

"She said she was trying to catch a stray cat," Brady noted.

"Then where was the cat?"

"Obviously, she didn't catch it."

"Obviously, there was no cat."

"C'mon, Coop." The two men turned onto Maple, nodded hello to Annabelle Scanlon opening up the post office. "What deep, dark secret could Caroline Benning possibly be hiding?"

"That's what I intend to find out."

Brady didn't doubt it. Coop was good at finding things out. It'd taken him less than two months to find out about Violet's death. Less than two months to answer the question Brady had secretly wondered for twenty-three years: *When is my mother coming home?* Now he knew. Never.

"Don't you trust anybody?" Brady asked.

Coop looked at him, one dark brow arching. They both knew it was the pot calling the kettle black. "Occupational hazard, Doc."

They walked a few more steps. Coop shrugged. "Maybe I'm wrong."

Brady saw the strong set of Coop's profile and knew the other man didn't believe he was mistaken about Caroline Benning.

"No wonder you haven't found your Woman of the River yet," Brady said, referring to the local story of Coop's ancestor and namesake, Night Hawk, whose dream of a hawk eventually led him to his own true love. "You think every woman you meet is Mata Hari."

Coop shifted his impenetrable gaze to Brady. Everyone knew the story of Coop's ancestor. Everyone also knew Coop believed the legend was just that—a legend. Nothing more.

"It's bad enough every time I see your brothers, I have to listen to them go on about the wonders of married life and watch them get all sentimental and sloppy," he said, "but at least I thought I could count on you to stay sane and steer clear of all this mush."

He glanced down at the flowered canister Brady was carrying. Some of his smile returned. "But what can I expect from a man who spends his free time making cookies for the hospital bake sale?"

"Bake sale? These cookies are mine, and I'm not sharing them with anyone, so stop angling for a handout."

Coop studied the tin. "Must be pretty special cookies. When did you take home ec?"

"I didn't make these cookies. They were given to me by a friend."

"I see..." Coop mused, contemplating the tin.

Brady saw his friend's speculative gaze. "What now, Columbo?"

Coop looked at him. "When did you start going for the Betty Crocker type? All the women I've seen you with are serious career gals whose idea of a gourmet meal comes with a waiter."

"I didn't say I was dating this woman. I said we were friends."

Coop laughed, dismissing Brady's answer.

Brady stopped in the middle of the sidewalk. "You don't believe me?"

"Sure, I believe you." Laughter was still traced in the strong lines of the young man's face.

"No, you don't." Brady's good mood was fading.

Coop eyed the canister. "You're not going to give me a cookie now, are you?"

Unsmiling, Brady lifted the tin's lid and grudgingly held out the cookies. Coop took a handful. He tipped his head in the direction of First Street. "Gotta go. See you Sunday at your dad's."

Brady nodded. Coop started toward the police substation. Brady knew the other man's skepticism was justified. Brady's many relationships with women weren't for friendship. They were for fun, relaxation and mutually agreed-on good, clean sex. No strings, no soul searching, no complications. It was the way he—and the women he dated—preferred it. In fact, he maintained a comfortable distance in all his personal and professional relationships.

Except for Eden. She had only to tilt her head and smile and it seemed he had no secrets. It had never been that way with anyone before.

"Hey, Brady," Coop called. Chewing, he held up a half-eaten cookie. "Marry this woman." With a rare laugh, he turned and continued down First Street.

MOLLY SPENCER balanced a stuffed rabbit in each hand. "These bunnies are so cute. When did you get them in?"

"Just yesterday." Eden came over to the wicker étagère. "There'll be more coming in a few days."

Molly put one bunny down and took a cookie from the plate Eden offered. "Good thing Sara isn't with me. She'd want one in every color." She pressed a butter-yellow bunny to her cheek. "I don't think I can resist this one, though. I'll put it away for her Easter basket."

"Goodness, they are adorable," Anna Kelsey agreed as she joined the women. She picked up a sky-blue bunny. "You have the nicest things, Eden. And the loveliest shop. So pleasant. Not to mention these fabulous cookies," she added as she took one. "It's so generous of you to make the floral decorations for Jenna's baby shower."

"It's my pleasure. Why don't we sit and have a cup of tea?" She indicated the small wrought-iron table and chairs in the corner. Nearby a tea cart offered all the fixings. "I'll bring over some books for you to look at, and we can figure out exactly what colors and flowers you'd like."

Anna looked at Molly. "Do we have time before we have to pick up the kids from Kaity's?"

Molly glanced at her watch. "Sure, we've got a few minutes."

"Good. And I think I'll bring this little fella with me." Anna carried the stuffed animal to the table. She smiled down into the bunny's eyes, the same brilliant blue as her own. "I'll save it for Jeremy's basket."

Molly set her purse on the chair and went to the tea cart. "Easter?" She smiled and winked at Eden. "Ten to one, Jeremy will have that bunny before lunch."

Anna settled into a chair. "Grandma is my name. Spoiling is my game."

Laughing, Molly brought the older woman a cup of tea.

"What?" Anna stirred sugar into her tea.

"You're trying to tell me that Sara isn't getting spoiled by that new daddy of hers?"

A loving curve came to Molly's lips at the mention of her new husband, Quinn.

"And what about those new uncles of hers?" Anna noted. "Why, Brady stood on that sidewalk right out there two nights ago and told me that Sara is 'pure adorable.'" She took another cookie. "Eden, you've got to give me the recipe for these. They're wonderful."

"You saw Brady the other night?" Molly sat down at the table.

"Let me get those books to give you some ideas what we can do for Jenna's shower," Eden suggested.

Anna nodded in response to Molly's question. "Yes. My mother had come over for pot roast, and it was such a lovely evening, Mom insisted on walking back to Worthington House. Eighty-seven, and I swear the woman has more energy than a teenager." Anna sipped her tea. "She doesn't miss a trick, either."

"We haven't seen much of Brady lately." Molly tapped her spoon on the edge of the cup, then set it on the saucer. "He doesn't dare miss Sunday night dinners at Quinn's father's, of course. Elias would write him out of the will. But even then he seems, well, preoccupied. Quinn says that's just Brady." She broke a cookie in half. "Of course, he knows him better than I, but I still say something's bothering him."

"You know, the other night he did seem a little odd." Anna nibbled on a cookie. "He appeared out of nowhere. Came out of the alley right next to the shop here. Scared the pudding out of me. Didn't faze Mom a bit. Just gave her more ammo to tease him with."

Eden returned to the table with several books. "Why don't we start with these? There's some wonderful ideas in them, but I have more books if you don't see anything you like here."

"What was he doing in the alley?" Molly took a book from the top of the stack but didn't open it.

"He didn't say," Anna replied. "I assumed he was on his way home from the hospital. He walks all the time no matter what the weather." Anna smiled at Eden. "He didn't stop in here to pick out some posies, did he?"

Eden opened the book Molly had selected and pointed to a picture. "Do you like this? See how the baskets are made to look like cradles?"

"Brady in a flower shop?" Molly smiled. "Wouldn't that be something like a bull in a china shop?"

Anna chuckled in agreement. "I do love the boy, but we all know he's not exactly the hearts-and-flowers type."

"He's a great doctor, though. He was wonderful with Sara that time she had the flu."

"He's one of Tyler's best surgeons. The people around here trust him. The doctors and nurses respect him. So, he may not win Mr. Congeniality.

Everybody knows beneath that no-nonsense attitude is a compassionate heart. Handholding doesn't put people back on their feet. Although he did give Mom a big buss on the cheek the other night. I don't know which one of them was more surprised.''

Molly looked at the other woman. "See what I mean? That's what I'm talking about. If I hadn't seen him lately, I wouldn't believe it, either. But I don't know. The man is acting peculiar."

Anna sipped her tea. "Well, maybe not so much peculiar as—what did you say earlier—preoccupied?"

Molly nodded.

"It's probably stress. He has a billion things on his mind, and it's only natural he sometimes gets as absentminded as the rest of us mortals. I'm sure that's what it was the other night when he seemed so confused."

"Confused?" Molly questioned.

"As if he didn't know which way he was going," Anna explained. "He came out of the alley, turned one way, walked a few steps, stopped, started again, stopped. Then he spun around and came our way."

"Maybe we should pick the color theme first. How about yellow or pink, blue, lavender?" Eden suggested. "Or did you have a specific flower preference?"

Molly glanced at the photo in the book opened on the table, but she said, "Quinn said Brady was born a doctor."

"Well, he always did have a grown-up air about

him, even when he was a youngster. Didn't he, Eden?'' Anna didn't wait for a reply. ''Of course, he had to grow up in a hurry. All the boys did after Violet ran off. It's not really my place to say, but I don't think it ever helped that Elias wouldn't talk to them about it.''

Molly nodded. The two other women knew she was thinking of her own husband and how she'd almost lost him to the past.

''In my opinion it would've done those boys some good to talk about it, but Elias didn't allow it. Violet was gone, and that was that. They had to deal with it. As the middle child, Brady always was the bridge between the two other boys, but after Violet left, he really took on the role of the family fixer. He tried to take care of everyone.'' Anna glanced at Eden. ''You were probably too young to remember.''

No, she remembered. She remembered the lines already etched in his brow, his face too solemn for a teen, as he'd blotted the blood off her scraped knees. She remembered him caught somewhere between boyhood and manhood, already trying to heal the world around him.

Anna chewed thoughtfully. ''He's a good man.'' She looked at Eden again for confirmation.

Eden nodded.

''Mom sure gave the poor fella a heck of a time the other night.'' Anna smiled at the memory. ''Wanted to know when he was going to come to his senses like his brothers did and settle down, start a family.''

''I'm sure he'd have no trouble finding a candidate. Lord knows, he's interviewed enough of them.'' Molly winked at the women.

''Is that what you young people are calling it nowadays?'' Anna still smiled. ''From the impression I got the other night, he seems bound and determined to keep his status as the last single Spencer brother.''

''The right girl hasn't come along yet, that's all.'' Molly touched the corners of her mouth with one of the linen napkins Eden always had folded in a small basket. ''And she's obviously not here in Tyler because he knows every available girl in town and has dated over half of them.''

''He does get around, but I bet he ends up with someone not from Tyler. Someone like that city doctor he was seeing a while back. That's the only relationship I think he's had that has lasted longer than a date or two.''

Molly stirred her tea. ''Maybe Jenna has some friends or cousins back in New York City? You can't get much more big city than that.''

''Well, whoever she is and wherever she comes from, I'll bet when the right girl comes along, Dr. Brady Spencer will fall like a sack of bricks.'' Anna winked at Molly. ''Just like his brothers.''

Eden stood, her chair scraping against the tiles. The other women looked at her. ''I'll get you both some more tea,'' she offered.

"Goodness, no." Molly glanced at her watch. "I'd love some, but it's almost time to pick up the kids and we haven't even looked at the flowers." She slid the opened book toward Anna. "This is pretty, isn't it?"

Eden carried her cup to the cart, straightened the china, lined up the silver spoons, waited for the roil of emotions within her to calm. She knew everything the women had said was the truth. Brady may not have found the right woman yet, but when he did, she would be sophisticated and dynamic, his equal in terms of experience, affluence and professional background. She wouldn't be a twenty-seven-year-old virgin whose most serious relationship to date had been with a cat.

"I like this with all the baby's breath and the Easter egg colors," Eden heard Anna say behind her.

Not that anyone in Tyler would consider that the attractive, seductive Dr. Spencer would ever be interested in someone like her. Eden tucked in the corner of a napkin. Even she knew her fantasies were ludicrous, had told herself hundreds of times. Anna and Molly would be shocked if they even suspected she entertained such thoughts. Brady Spencer and Eden Frazier? Preposterous.

"We really only need a large centerpiece for the buffet table," Anna said, "and a few smaller arrangements for the cake table. These cradle-looking baskets Eden showed us are nice."

"Maybe some type of floral favors? What do you think, Eden?" Molly asked.

What did she think? At that particular moment she was thinking how just once she'd like to be thought of as more than good ol' Eden, as constant and predictable as Timber Lake's spring rising...and about half as exciting.

Chapter Three

"We're friends, aren't we, Eden?"

She went still, the cookies she'd been about to put with the others in the napkin-lined basket hovering. She knew the tone. She'd known it all her life. *You're a pal, Eden...a good kid.... I can talk to you as if you were one of the guys.... You're like a sister to me.*

She glanced behind her. Brady sat at the kitchen table. He looked tired tonight. She shouldn't have kept him so long last night, plying him with cookies and cups of tea, but she had so loved sitting across from him, hearing his voice, watching his features change, seeing him smile.

He'd come late again tonight to order another arrangement. He'd also brought back her empty cookie tin. Even before he'd grumbled about having to share the contents with half the town, she'd already suspected he hoped she would fill the tin again. She'd opened it to do just that and found first aid supplies. She'd looked questioningly at him.

"My moth—" He'd caught himself and began again. "We were taught never to return a container empty."

She'd looked at the gauze pads, the tube of triple antibiotic ointment, the box of butterfly closures.

"It's something you can always use. You never know when you might have an emergency."

His voice had been so earnest and sincere, she'd had to smile. Who needed diamonds and Godiva chocolates when you had sterile gauze pads in a variety of sizes?

Now Brady waited for an answer to the question he'd just asked. Despite his fatigue, his green eyes didn't miss their mark. She put the cookies in the basket. "I like to think of you as a friend, Brady."

She saw his features relax, and her own worries grew. She'd thought she'd been careful. Had she, somehow, revealed to Brady how attracted she was to him? Had he sensed she dreamed of more, much more than friendship? Was he now attempting to let her down easy?

"And friends who bring you first aid...well, they're rare." She smiled at him, trying to postpone what she feared was inevitable. She knew the routine. She'd heard it before. *I like you, Eden. I really do. You're a great girl. It's just that I don't like you in that way. But we can still be friends, can't we?*

She brought the basket to the table. Brady's face was pensive, weary. She'd take friendship. Except for her fantasies, she'd never expected more.

"You look beat tonight."

He smiled, but even his eyes now had the unfocused look of someone who needed sleep. She picked up the basket. "Why don't we sit in the living room? You'll be more comfortable on the couch. We can have our cookies and tea in there at the coffee table."

She led the way into the room painted soft apricot and cozy with plants and plump pillows. She cleared off the cedar chest that had been passed on to her by her parents when they'd retired and moved to Florida. She set the basket on the chest.

"I'll just get some plates and napkins."

"Let me help you."

She shook her head. "You make yourself comfortable. I'll be right back."

He started to sit, but when she returned, he was standing across the room, looking at the painting that leaned against the wall.

"That's not finished yet," she said.

"You painted this?" He picked up the canvas, held it at arm's length and examined its vibrant color splashes, its heavy black shapes, its strong assault on the senses.

"It's a hobby." She dismissed the work, embarrassed and self-conscious. She set down the plates and napkins. "I'll bet you didn't eat anything again today. Come have a cookie." She tried to lure him away from the painting.

"I don't know much about art—"

"Neither do I."

He looked at her, his eyes once again intent. "You've had no formal training?"

"Some appreciation classes in college, but my major was horticulture, of course. Like I said, it's just something I do."

"Really?" Brady looked at the painting. "I like it."

She sat in the rocking chair next to the sofa. "You do?"

He propped the canvas against the wall and stepped back, studying the painting. "I like it a lot." He looked at her.

Perched on the chair's seat, she felt as if he could see right through her. She touched her throat above her buttoned collar. The kettle on the stove whistled.

She jumped up, grateful to get away from Brady's gaze. "Tea's ready," she sang out too loud. "Peppermint? Cinnamon apple?"

"Peppermint's fine," he answered, his eyes still on her as she went into the kitchen.

She gathered the tea things and carried them on a tray back into the living room. Brady had picked up the painting again.

"Do you have any more?"

She stopped. "Any more?"

"Paintings."

"Why?"

He smiled. It was the smile the others talked about—the smile they said could save lives.

"I'd like to see some more."

She looked at the strong shapes, textures, the

powerful mix of primary tones on the rectangle in his hands. It was a hobby, something she did when her quiet world got too quiet and the perfect balance, careful symmetry of her arrangements made her shake. She would bring out her canvases, her darkest, richest colors, and brushes so soft to the touch she had to close her eyes and rub them across her lids.

She hadn't been allowed to paint as a child. Crayons were okay; paints were too messy for parents used to a serene, orderly household. No being loud, running, banging, acting like a baby, being silly. Not only did that type of behavior disrupt the household, but Eden could get hurt. Her mother, having longed for her for so long, had been especially overprotective, spying potential dangers everywhere. By the time Eden went to school, her natural timidity had become a deeply ingrained shyness. Uneasy around people, strange places, unfamiliar experiences, she created her own imaginary world. There she was safe.

Eventually the extreme fearfulness and shyness had shifted into a content quietness, a dignified reserve. The world she had once only envisioned in her head was now real. Flowers always bloomed, people always smiled, nothing evil or hurtful was allowed. And the quiet that had been born in her and entrenched by experience was tolerated, welcome even, and only occasionally painful.

It was then, when longing became pain, that she locked her apartment door and went to her paints.

Brush in hand, she became someone else—someone wild, loud, spontaneous, shocking. She painted, and she was free.

She'd never shown the paintings to anyone.

Holding the canvas, Brady waited for her answer. The lights in his dark-brown hair were as strong as the deepest color in her painting.

She set the tray on the cedar chest. "Just a moment."

She went into her bedroom and kneeled by the canopy bed with the Battenburg lace duvet and the Victorian doll propped against the pillows. She lifted the bedskirt and saw the canvases lying there in the dark. She pulled them out. Some were smaller than others; all were passionate and intense. The work of a woman possessed, Eden thought, sitting back on her haunches, once more hesitating.

"I like that one. That one, too."

She started, not having heard Brady come in. She looked over her shoulder and saw him leaning against the doorjamb.

"May I?" He looked not at her but the paintings.

She stood, brushed off her creased pants. Brady, not waiting for her answer, came and stood next to her. Together they looked at the colors and contrasts and textures and shapes spread out across the floor like a madwoman's quilt. She felt him beside her more keenly than if she were in his embrace.

He picked up a smaller one and brushed off the dust that clung to its thick edges. "Why do you hide them under your bed?"

She didn't meet his eyes. "They're only a hobby."

They both knew they were much more than that.

He turned the canvas over. "You don't sign them?"

He was too near. She was too exposed. She looked away from the brilliant colors and found his eyes on her. "The tea's getting cold."

He smiled. "Yes, the tea." His fingertip followed a ridge in the painting where the color had been applied thick and fast. He laid it next to the others. "Thank you for showing them to me."

"You're welcome." The words were stiff; her voice a schoolmarm's. "Shall we go have our tea?"

"Can I help you put them away?"

"No." The answer was firm. "I'll do it later."

"Are you sure?"

She nodded. He looked at her but didn't ask again.

She followed him into the living room, turning off the bedroom light, leaving the paintings in darkness.

She sat on the hard seat of the rocking chair, leaning forward to pass Brady his tea. He took the mug from her hand, his fingers meeting the tips of hers. A current moved up her arm from his touch. She pulled her hand away. Stop being silly, she told herself.

She straightened in the wood seat, balancing her mug on her thigh. She tried a tiny smile, added some small talk. "Anna Kelsey and Molly came in today."

"Oh." He leaned against the back of the sofa, resting his elbow on the upholstered arm, his mug held in his wide hand. He shifted toward her, stretching one leg diagonally across the couch so that his foot dangled. His other arm extended and stretched along the sofa's back.

"They came in to choose the decorations for Jenna's baby shower—a floral arrangement for the buffet table, some favors, balloons, that kind of thing."

He nodded. She was boring him. "Anna mentioned she ran into you the other night outside the shop."

He smiled, but the tiredness she'd seen earlier in his face deepened. "She was walking Martha home to Worthington House."

"She said Martha gave you a hard time."

He nodded again. "She's trying to scare up another couple ready for a wedding present. The Quilting Circle must need a new project." He leaned forward to set his tea on the chest, then sat back, stretching his arms over his head. "I told her the Spencer family has already done their share for a few years." He settled into the couch. "I should've never sat down."

He straightened, pressing his palms against the seat cushions. He shook his head apologetically, his eyes heavy-lidded. "I've got to go, Eden, before I fall asleep right here."

"Of course." She jumped up from the chair. "Let me just wrap up some cookies for you to take home." She put the basket on the tea tray and carried it into the kitchen.

She opened a cupboard and took out another tin like the one Brady had returned this evening.

"You can warm them in the microwave and they'll taste like they just came out of the oven." She piled the cookies in the tin and pushed down the lid as she walked into the living room. "I gave you all the cookies I had in case you have to share."

She heard a snore. "Brady?"

He had settled into the sofa, his leg propped up, his arm outstretched. His head had fallen back, his mouth parted.

"Brady?"

He snored again.

She should wake him. But as she was about to touch his shoulder, he snored. She snatched her hand away.

"Brady?" Her whisper was urgent.

He shifted onto his side and brought both legs up on the cushions. The side of his face pressed against the needlepoint pillow propped against the sofa's arm.

She really should wake him. Her hand reached out again to lightly tap his shoulder. He shifted once more, only to burrow his body deeper into the cushions.

Eden retreated to the rocking chair. She rocked, watching him. His body was too long to stretch out fully and so was tucked, the knees bent, the arms folded across his chest. His snores were rhythmic now, a deep, full bass that sounded of authority even as he slept. His mouth had opened but was not slack. None of the strong lines, the flat planes of his face had softened. She rocked back and forth and wondered if this solid, self-reliant man ever rested.

His body turned again as if searching for comfort. His shoulders were as wide as the couch. One hand fell from its tight press to his chest. It lay against his leg, the fingers unfurling, reaching, the palm exposed, and that hand that had healed so many was at rest.

She couldn't wake him now. She wasn't bold enough to slip off his shoes, but she did take the crocheted afghan out of the wicker basket in the corner and unfold it, letting it fall across his body. Some fringe fell on his chin, across his opened mouth. She brushed the yarn away, careful not to touch him.

She took another afghan from the basket and, wrapping it around herself, sat back in the rocker. What harm would it do, she thought as she rocked gently, if Brady rested a few hours on her couch? No one knew he was here. And even if they did, no one would ever assume anything inappropriate was going on between the handsome doctor and herself. Anna and Molly's conversation had confirmed that fact today, but even before, Eden had known. The idea that someone like Brady would be attracted to someone like Eden would never cross anyone's mind in Tyler…except maybe in Eden's imaginings. And even she knew it was only a dream. Her dream.

She switched off the lights in the living room and the kitchen and, pulling the afghan tighter around her, walked to her bedroom, closing the door behind her. She didn't turn on the overhead light. She didn't want to see the paintings lying extravagantly across the carpet. She was unable to undress, even in the dark. She lay down on the bed, completely clothed, the afghan wrapped around her.

She closed her eyes. Let him sleep, she thought. And she would dream.

SOMETHING HIT HIM square in the center of Brady's groin. He bolted upright, exclaiming, "No going below the belt."

Two glassy orange eyes floated before him. A fear he hadn't experienced since he saw Linda Blair's head do a three-sixty in *The Exorcist* washed through him. The glowing eyes blinked as a weight settled across his pelvis.

"Listen," he told the copper mirrors, "if this is an alien body snatching, you can take any part of my body but that."

The weight lifted. "I'm glad you see my side of this." The orange ovals came toward him until something tickled his skin where he'd unbuttoned his collar when he'd gotten to Eden's last night.

Eden's? He stared into the metallic eyes, his own eyes adjusting to the darkness. "Penelope? What are you doing here?"

He looked around, saw the long, black shape of the cedar chest, the round tin on top of it. He could almost make out the lace curtains, the night black beyond them. He lifted Penelope off his lap onto the floor. His own feet hit the rug.

"More precisely, what am *I* doing here?"

He stood, careful not to make any noise and tried to remember. Was there anything he should remember? There'd been the paintings, the colors rich and evocative and so unlike Eden. There'd been the cookies and the mild tea. There'd been an overwhelming fatigue that had turned into a deep contentment as he'd sat in Eden's living room, surrounded by warm, soothing aromas and gentle colors.

He must've fallen asleep, and Eden, being Eden, had kindly let him sleep. He folded the blanket and lay it across the back of the couch. He considered writing a note but didn't want to turn on a light and risk waking his hostess. Instead he felt his way to the kitchen. As he opened the door that led to the stairs, he heard something behind him. He looked back, half hoping to see Eden, still soft and warm from sleep, coming toward him. Instead Penelope padded across the kitchen and stared at him, the dilated black of her pupils accusing.

"Listen, Penelope, if I had any intentions at all, they'd be honorable." He closed the door on the animal's incriminating gaze. He tiptoed down the stairs, wondering why he was explaining himself to a cat.

The darkness was deeply shadowed as he stepped outside. Standing on the welcome mat on the back step, he stretched, stiff from sleeping on the small sofa. He stepped into the alley and heard a rumble behind him. He looked over his shoulder and was caught in a sweep of blinding light. He shaded his forehead against the glare, enough to make out the shape of a large truck idling in front of him.

"Hey, Doc." Herb Smythe leaned out of the truck cab's window.

Brady stepped out of the glare, closer to the cab. The Wild, Wild Waste Company was emblazoned across the truck's door. Above it Herb was chewing on an unlit cigar stub. His baseball hat read, "Don't hate me because I'm beautiful."

"What brings you out this early, Doc?"

Brady tried to decipher Herb's expression. He didn't think the man had seen him coming out of Eden's place at this early hour, but he wasn't sure. Not that anything inappropriate had happened, but still, rumors only ranked behind the annual monster truck exhibitions as favorite forms of entertainment in this small town.

"You know what they say, Herb. Early bird gets the worm."

"Yeah?" Herb smiled, the cigar clamped between his teeth. "Then how come I only get garbage?" He downshifted, easing the truck back toward the Dumpster behind The Hair Affair. He leaned out the cab window again, shifting the cigar stub to the other side of his mouth. "If you were hoping to catch me with this cigar lit, you're wasting your time. Three months now it's been."

Brady patted the truck's side. "Glad to hear it, Herb."

"The missus says I'm grouchy as a grizzly woken in January, but she never did like me much, anyway." Herb grinned once more. "Say, you must be next in line to take the plunge since your brothers up and got hitched."

Brady shook his head. "Don't start shining your two-stepping shoes yet."

Herb's eyebrows met the bill of his cap. "No? I've heard that before. Then the next thing I know, I'm buying Irene a new hat and raising shots of Jim Beam to the groom."

"It won't be me, Herb."

"You're still in it for the sport then, huh, Doc?" Herb's question followed Brady as he headed down the alley.

Brady raised his hand goodbye. "You just keep that cigar unlit, Herb, because you're going to have to live a long time if you want to dance at my wedding."

WHEN EDEN WOKE, her first thought was, Is he gone? She had never before woken up to wonder if a man still slept on her sofa. She wasn't sure what she wanted the answer to be.

She swung her legs over the side of the bed and sat up. She was still fully dressed except for her socks, which never stayed up and had slipped off her feet sometime during the night. She slid her bare feet into her slippers and stood. As she walked to the door, she stepped over her paintings, their colors garish in the morning light. She glanced in the mirror above her bureau, her own pale face equally harsh in the morning glare. She rubbed the sleepers out of her eyes, patted her cheeks, ran a brush through her hair until it lay straight. She practiced a bright smile in the mirror, blinking her eyes several times as if she could make them sparkle. "Good morning, Brady," she whispered through her full smile. "Sleep well?" She looked at herself in the mirror. Her smile dissolved, her shoulders rounded. "Please don't let him be here," she prayed.

She took a deep breath, split her face with a sunny smile and opened the door.

Stretched out where Brady had lain was only Penelope. The Persian raised her head as the door opened, saw it was Eden and, with an annoyed twitch of her whiskers, went back to sleep.

Eden's smile again disappeared and her shoulders slumped. She looked down, saw the giant bumblebee slippers on her feet. Usually they made her smile. Today, knowing they were the wildest things she'd probably ever wear, they brought tears to her eyes.

She pressed her wrists to her eyes and rubbed. Today was Saturday. Her shipment from the wholesaler would be here within the hour. The flowers had to be unpacked and processed. Stock containers had to be stuffed and filled with water and preservative.

The Breakfast Inn Bed's standing weekly order of arrangements had to be finished and delivered before afternoon check-in time. There was another one of those strange conventions up at the Timberlake Lodge again this weekend and fifteen table arrangements of nightshade and witch hazel had been ordered for their awards dinner tonight. There would be the usual Saturday array of get-well arrangements, happy birthday bouquets and over-the-counter sales of "first date" flowers. There would be walk-ins, call-ins and wire orders. And before it all began, Eden had to get to the bank this morning. Afraid she'd miss Brady yesterday, she'd decided to wait until the bank opened this morning to deposit the daily receipts and get change for today. She also had to stop at the post office which, like the bank, closed at noon on Saturdays.

She padded into the kitchen and put the kettle on. She stood at the stove, watching morning make its way through the curtains. No, there was no time for tears today.

She was downstairs, finishing the arrangements for the Breakfast Inn Bed by the time Christy arrived. The teenager held up a bakery box as she came in through the back. "I brought you some of Mom's pastries."

Christy Hanson's mom, Britt Marshack, had founded one of Tyler's most successful private companies, YES! Yogurt, which she and her husband, Jake, operated on Britt's family farm. But Britt was equally famous around Tyler for her pastries, which she made primarily for her best friend, Marge, to sell at her diner.

"And I brought extra for the shop." Christy put the box on the tea cart and reached for a plate on the shelf underneath. Christy was Britt's daughter from her first marriage and had worked for Eden after school three days a week and on Saturday since she was sixteen. Eden was going to miss her when she left for college next fall. Fortunately, her brother, David, who did deliveries after school and on the weekends, would still be around a few years.

"You must've read my mind. I was just thinking I'd better pick something up at the store when I'm out this morning. I...I didn't have time to bake yesterday," she lied. The tin of cookies she'd fixed for Brady still sat on the cedar chest in her living room where he left it.

"Been busy, huh?" Christy smiled as she arranged the pastries.

"Well, I did have time to bake earlier in the week, but those cookies are gone."

"From what I hear, your cookies are getting as popular as Mom's pastries." Still smiling, Christy gave Eden a sidelong glance. "When I dropped off Marge's order at the diner this morning, she said Deputy Night Hawk was raving about them over his morning coffee. And everybody knows it takes a lot to get the deputy excited."

"Cooper?" Eden looked at Christy, puzzled. "He hasn't been in the shop that I remember. I wonder how he would've gotten hold of my cookies?"

Christy brought the plate to Eden. "I wonder." Her smile stayed. Her voice was playful. "Maybe somebody gave him one?"

"I suppose." Eden selected a pastry. Her employee continued to stand in front of her, grinning so widely her nose crinkled, adding to her impish charm. "Christy, is everything okay?"

"Super. How's everything been with you?"

"Fine." She warily regarded the girl. "I've got to run out to the bank and the post office before they close."

"Okeydoke." Christy didn't move.

"I'll be back before it gets busy in here. You know what to do—make up some boxes, stock the design table, put together some net puffs, make up some bows."

Christy nodded. Her smiling lips pressed together as if she were about to burst. Merriment danced in her eyes, earning her further study from Eden before she turned to leave. Halfway across the showroom, she turned back. "Christy?"

The girl was arranging the tea cart, the cat-who-ate-the-canary smile still on her face.

"Is there something you want to share with me?"

"No. Is there something you'd like to share with me?"

"No." Eden gave the girl one last puzzled look. "I'll be right back."

"Okay," Christy sang out. "I'll be here."

Eden wondered about Christy's odd behavior as

she crossed to the square. She swallowed the last bite of her pastry and shrugged. *Teenagers.*

She crossed again at the opposite side of the square, admiring the new displays in the Gates Department Store windows as she passed. At the post office, Annabelle stopped sorting mail and called her over to the counter for a chat. After a few pleasantries, the conversation turned into more of a question-and-answer session concerning Eden's recent activities. Fortunately, a customer came in to buy stamps, and Eden was able to escape without appearing rude. As she hurried to the bank two blocks over, she couldn't help but wonder about Annabelle's sudden, almost prying, interest in Eden's life. Normally no one noticed her.

By the time she reached the bank's lobby, she'd decided Annabelle was only being amiable. As she followed the red carpet to where the tellers sat behind a high counter, she told herself she should be ashamed for suspecting the woman's friendly overtures. Past the teller area, framed by glass partitions, were offices. Outside his office Eden saw Seth Spencer, president of the Tyler Savings & Loan.

"How you doing, Irene?" Eden slid the deposit bag toward the teller. "I'll need change, too."

Past Irene's shoulder, she saw Seth glance toward the teller area.

"How's Herb?" She returned her attention to the middle-aged woman.

"As big a pain as ever." Irene Smythe counted the deposits. "Less than tolerable since he gave up smoking those nasty cigars." She winked. "But a hair more healthy."

"Gave up smoking his cigars, huh? Never thought I'd hear that." Something made her glance toward the offices again. Seth was staring at her. She knew him only by face and name, but not wanting to appear unfriendly, she raised her hand and waved.

He nodded, looked thoughtfully at her a second more before turning back into his office.

Irene swiveled in her chair to see whom Eden was waving to. When she turned back, her smile had an unsettling resemblance to Christy's this morning.

"Yes, Herb's feeling mighty better since he swore off those cigars. Although, he'll never admit it."

Eden unzipped the money pouch and put the deposit receipt inside. "I'm glad to hear it." She handed Irene several large bills. "Just the usual."

Irene counted the bills into the cash drawer, exchanging them for smaller currency. "I have Doc Spencer to thank. He's the one who convinced Herb to give up the cigars one day when Herb had to have a mole removed. It wasn't cancerous, thank the Lord, but it was a bit of a scare. That plus Doc Spencer's lecture on smoking as the number one cause of lung cancer along with other serious diseases was enough to make Herb think. Oh, he still chews on an unlit one when he's working. Says he'd be unbearable if he went cold turkey, and I'm inclined to agree, but it won't be long before he gives that up, too." She stacked Eden's money and pushed it across the counter. "He's a good man, Doc Spencer."

Eden heard the echo of Anna Kelsey's same words spoken yesterday in the shop. "That's what everybody says." She gathered the money and put it into the zippered pouch.

"I hear he's even started to make house calls now."

Eden looked up, saw the smile worn first by Christy, now Irene. Her own polite smile became baffled. *House calls?* Had someone seen Brady come into the flower shop after hours? Did they suspect Brady was the Flower Phantom and were trying to get Eden to confirm it? Gina had been pestering her since the deliveries began, but it was more like a game between the two good friends, since Gina knew Eden would never betray a trust. Still, was it possible that others who didn't know her so well were hoping she'd reveal the secret? Was that the reason why everyone was acting so odd?

What other reason could there be? If Brady had been seen coming and going from her place at odd hours, the only other assumption people could possibly make was that Brady and she were having an affair. Her smile widened at her wishful thinking.

She'd have to remember to tell Brady to be more careful if he didn't want his goodwill gestures to be found out. Until then, the best thing to do was to just smile. Her mouth curved as if she were the happiest woman in the world.

"I'd better get back. I left Christy all alone, and

Saturdays are always crazy." Her smile was so wide her cheeks began to hurt. "Take care, Irene. Give Herb my congrats on not smoking anymore. Tell him to keep up the good work."

She turned to go and saw Seth looking at her again, his expression so intense and curious, it stopped her. He averted his gaze as soon as she spied him. Still, surprise kept her standing there a few seconds longer. Finally she walked across the lobby and outside toward the sanctity of her shop. Then she remembered Christy's odd behavior. She looked back at the Tyler Savings & Loan. The brick building stood square and sturdy, its crowning clock tower counting the seconds. Past it, the brick and wooden fronts of the grocery store, drugstore and cleaners lined up along the oak-shaded Main Street. In the distance the Methodist Church bells tolled the hour, their chimes constant and comforting.

Everything in Tyler was the same as it'd always been. So why did it suddenly seem as if the whole town was acting strange?

Chapter Four

Supper was over, the dishes done. Dessert would be soon when stomachs settled. The day was graying, but the mild air had lingered, granting Elias Spencer and his family another half hour on the front porch. It had been a long winter as were all Wisconsin winters, and although jackets and sweaters were still necessary, it felt good to sit outside, rocking on the wide porch.

All Elias's sons were there, three born of his blood and one adopted by his heart. Four boys all different in looks as well as temperament. Seth, the oldest, was the analyst; Quinn, the youngest, was the charmer; Brady, the middle boy, was the giver; and the adopted son, Cooper, was the silent soul.

There were others, too. Seth and Quinn had taken wives. In November, Seth had married the wild but wise Jenna. She joined him on the porch now, standing beside his chair. He looked into her eyes, laying his hand on her stomach, full with their twin babies due in May.

Quinn had chosen Molly with her tiny figure and frail beauty and surprising will of iron. They had married mid-January. She played "Mother, May I?" on the sloping front lawn now with her young daughter from her first marriage, Sara. Quinn ambled off the porch, tapped Sara on the shoulder. "You're it," he said, jogging off slowly enough for her to catch him.

The other two boys were still single, although there was an edginess, a restlessness about them that was reminiscent of Seth and Quinn right before they stopped fighting themselves and fate.

It was Seth, made brave by love, who had asked Elias for permission to search for their mother. Twenty-three years ago Violet had left, and for twenty-three years Elias hadn't spoken her name. Nor had the boys in his presence.

Elias had said yes. The boys were men now. Twenty-three years ago he'd thought the silence would save them, save him. Now he wasn't so sure.

Not that Elias had spoken of this to them. His silence was a part of him now. Even when Cooper had discovered Violet had died in childbirth seven months after she'd run away, Elias hadn't spoken of her. Still the news had reverberated within them all. Even now its echo was there, low and constant, like the steady rocking of his chair. Fortunately, by the time the news had come, Seth had already made his choice to love and make peace with the past; Quinn, halfway there, had soon followed.

Elias leaned back, looked at his middle son sitting

beside him. Brady had always healed others. He would heal himself.

Elias looked at his other sons and their young wives. He saw Sara smiling and thought of the children to come. He folded his hands, rested them on his lap and rocked.

They were a family. Hopefully, one day they would all heal. It was time.

COOPER WAS PROPPED on the porch railing, his back resting on a pole, but his eyes, always vigilant, scanned the surroundings. His gaze settled on Quinn and Sara chasing each other, but his pensive expression revealed his thoughts were elsewhere.

"Jenna, you still see much of that new girl, the one who waitresses at Marge's?" Coop's gaze stayed on the front lawn. "Didn't you two become pretty good friends when you roomed at the boarding house?"

Jenna rested her hand on top of Seth's along the curve of her stomach. "Caroline? Sure, I run into her here and there, and I stop into the diner sometimes to say hi."

"And maybe have a piece of Marge's hot apple pie?" Seth looked at his wife, the love as obvious as the teasing in his eyes.

She patted his hand. "I'm eating for three, remember?" Love was in her eyes, too.

"How's she getting on in Tyler?" Cooper prompted.

Jenna's gaze met the deputy's dark one. "Fine, I guess. Why?"

He shrugged. "No particular reason. Just wondering how she's settling in."

Brady saw Jenna look at Seth, her eyes asking for an answer.

Now Seth shrugged. "Coop's got a feeling about her."

"A feeling?" Jenna shifted her gaze from her husband to his friend. Cooper was feigning interest once again in Sara and Quinn's tag game.

"A feeling?" Jenna looked again at her husband.

"Coop thinks Caroline is hiding something."

"Hiding something? Like what?" she asked both men.

"Nothing. Forget it," Coop said.

"Maybe she does act a little strange at times, but she's still the outsider in town," Jenna defended her friend. "She gets nervous."

Brady, stretched out in the chair next to his father, folded his hands on his full stomach. A rare contentment had filled him as he'd watched Quinn chase Sara, listened to his family's voices. His eyes were half-closed. "Can't the people of Tyler find something better to gossip about than Caroline Benning?"

The silence on the porch was unbroken except for his father's chair rocking and Sara's shouts from the front yard. It continued too long. Brady opened his eyes. The others looked away.

"What?"

Seth looked at him. "As a matter of fact, yes. The people of Tyler have found something else to talk about."

"Good." Brady lowered his lids to half-mast again. "I'm glad they've found something else to hold their interest."

"Are you sure?"

He reluctantly returned his gaze to his brother. "Why shouldn't I be? Now maybe everyone will give Caroline a break." He glanced at Cooper, surprised to see he was grinning. Seth, too, was smiling.

"Coffee's probably done," Jenna announced. "Anyone ready for dessert? Eva made a delicious-looking blueberry cobbler."

"What about you, Brady? You want some dessert?" Coop asked.

"Why not?" Brady eyed the man's smiling face. He knew Coop couldn't pass up one of Eva's desserts. Eva, Elias's housekeeper, made sure she prepared a full-course Sunday meal before she took off for the day.

"After all those cookies you ate this week?" Coop's grin widened. Seth chuckled.

Brady looked at his father. "You know what the joke is?"

Elias shook his head. "No, but the way these two are grinning like hyenas, I'm certain we'll find out soon."

"Home free," Quinn yelled, collapsing on the porch steps.

Sara pounced on him. "You're it!"

"Please have mercy on the old man. I'm thirty, you know."

Sara looked at her new daddy, her big eyes suddenly serious. "You *are* old," she said.

"Hey, you didn't have to agree." Quinn grabbed her around the waist and tickled her.

She gave a delighted yelp. "Mommy, help," she cried as Molly dropped on the steps next to Quinn.

"Sorry, honey," Molly said, taking deep breaths. "Your daddy's not the only one who's falling apart." She closed her eyes, resting her head on a step.

"Hey, Sara," Jenna said, "why don't you come with Aunt Jenna and help me put the whipped cream on the pie?"

"Sure." Sara jumped off Quinn.

"Extra on your daddy's now," he told her.

"Let me help you, too, Jenna." Molly pushed herself up off the steps. Quinn grabbed her hand, pulling her back down on top of him to give her a long kiss. When he finally released her, she looked at him with bright eyes, her fair skin tinted pink. "What was that for?"

"I'm making sure I get extra, extra whipped cream on my pie." Quinn smiled.

She lightly punched his chest as she rolled off him, but as she went inside, her smile mirrored his.

"Hey, Quinn, you know what the hot news everyone in town is talking about?" Brady looked at his brother.

Quinn looked at him, then at Seth and Cooper. He too smiled. "I'll give you a hint. It involves a certain florist."

Brady stared at his smiling brothers, his own expression turning serious. They knew. Somehow they'd found out he was the one behind all the anonymous flower deliveries, the balloon-a-grams, the baskets of cheer that seemed to arrive wherever needed. They knew he was the Flower Phantom.

"So, you know?"

His brothers and Cooper nodded.

If Brady was the type to blush, he would have been crimson right now. "The whole town knows?"

They nodded.

His whole professional career flashed before his eyes. He'd have to figure out later how to explain his unorthodox behavior to his colleagues and superiors. First, he had to face his family. He steeled himself, waiting for their jests.

Quinn got up and propped himself on the railing. "You don't have to look so worried. We think it's great."

Brady frowned. "You do?"

"Sure," Seth agreed.

Brady looked at Cooper, who nodded. "You didn't have to keep it a secret."

Brady looked from Coop to the others. He wasn't convinced he wasn't being set up. "Admit it. You guys had a good chuckle when you found out."

"I was surprised," Seth confessed.

Quinn and Cooper agreed.

"I mean, at first, who would have thought? But then after thinking about it, it made sense to me." Seth turned to the other two men. "Did it make sense to you guys after you thought about it?"

They nodded in unison.

Brady stared at them. How could it make sense to his brothers and Coop when he himself didn't understand his recent odd behavior?

"We're just glad you're happy," Coop assured him.

Was he happy?

"Would you boys mind telling me what the hell you're talking about?" Elias looked at his sons.

The uneasy relief Brady had felt evaporated. His father didn't know. What would he say? What would he think? This man who had never let on about his own feelings, who had taught his sons that strong men don't reveal themselves. What would he think when he learned Brady was secretly doling out daisies around town?

Elias eyed his son and waited. Brady was silent, trying to choose the right words.

"Go ahead," Quinn urged. "It's nothing to be shy about. We've all been there. It happens to the best of us."

Brady looked at his younger brother, not understanding now.

"Go ahead," Quinn prompted. "Tell him you're in love."

"What?" Brady and his father both exclaimed.

Jenna appeared at the screen door. "Pie and coffee are ready."

"Mmm, pie and coffee." Seth sprang up. Coop and Quinn followed.

"I better have extra whipped cream," Quinn warned.

"Forget about the extra whipped cream." It was the voice saved for the operating room, the voice never challenged.

The three men turned as one and looked at Brady.

"What are you talking about—I'm in love?"

"Okay, I was giving you the benefit of the doubt." Quinn looked at the others for aid. "So, it's only an affair like they say." He shook his head. "Some people aren't going to be happy about that. I mean, it's none of their business, and you're both consenting adults, but still, they might say you took advantage. You know how people like to talk."

"And they are talking about it," Seth added.

"Talking about *it?* What's *it?*" Brady's voice rose in exasperation.

"You and Eden Frazier playing doctor."

"*What?* Me? Eden Frazier? Playing doctor?" Brady regarded the others, completely incredulous.

"Wait a minute. You just said yourself it was true," Seth pointed out. "You asked us how we found out."

"I didn't know you were talking about Eden and I and…" Brady waved his hands. "The whole thing's ridiculous."

"So, you aren't having an affair with Eden?" Cooper asked.

"No." Brady rubbed his brow where the lines had deepened.

"Then who are you playing doctor with?" Cooper—and the others—waited for an answer.

Brady tried to keep his voice calm. "No one." Their expressions became skeptical. "You don't believe me?"

"The rumors are flying all over town."

Brady slammed his palm against the chair arm. "And you believe them? All of you? You believe them?" He bolted out of the chair and paced the long porch.

"If you say it's not true, we believe you, Brady," Seth reassured him. "But it's not going to be that easy to convince the rest of the town. This is juicy stuff, you know—sweet, shy, innocent Eden and the handsome Dr. Meet-and-Mate."

Brady spun around, looked at the others. "Dr. Meet-and-Mate?"

Quinn shrugged. "People are going to talk."

"Dr. Meet-and-Mate?" Brady repeated too evenly.

"It's just a nickname some of the nurses gave you." Seth couldn't help smiling. "You know, because you see a lot of women but no one ever gets close to you. Except physically, of course."

"The one I heard was Dr. Divine," Quinn offered. "Because you're untouchable."

Brady shot his brother a sharp glance.

Elias had stopped rocking. He looked at his son. "Brady, are you romantically involved with Eden Frazier?"

Brady's gaze moved from one man to another, but he thought of Eden—her comforting smile, the way she tilted her head toward him as he talked, her world like a respite from all other reality. He remembered her paintings, promising a woman of deep passion and need.

"No, I'm not involved with Eden Frazier." The words felt like a lie. He turned to Cooper. "You see, this is what I was talking about the other morning. One person makes a comment, another person overhears it and the next thing you know the whole town is talking. Things get exaggerated, misunderstood." He rubbed his brow. "People get hurt."

His brothers and Coop consulted each other silently.

"Then you didn't spend the night at her house Friday?" Seth asked.

Brady gaped at his brother. "How'd you know that?" he said, revealing himself, but he already remembered Herb Smythe seeing him in the shop's alleyway Saturday morning. He remembered Martha Bauer's sharp gaze the night he'd run into her and her daughter outside The Garden of Eden. How many other people had seen him coming and going into Eden's shop after-hours through the back door like some kind of...lover?

"So, you did spend Friday night at Eden's place?" Quinn the lawyer cross-examined.

"It's not what it looks like," Brady tried to explain. "I was at her place. We got to talking. It got late. I fell asleep on her couch. Eden knew how tired I was and let me sleep."

Even to his ears, it sounded flimsy. Yet it was the truth. He'd been tired, and Eden had been kind to him, had let him rest. And he'd slept like a man who wasn't afraid to dream.

Now he had ruined her reputation. His misery multiplied.

"I slept on the couch. She slept in her bed. I woke up before dawn and left. She was still sleeping. I haven't even talked to her since." He watched the men's faces, gauging their acceptance of the truth.

Coop, always the detective, said, "I didn't even know you knew Eden Frazier beyond a casual 'how-do-you-do?'"

"I don't know her that well." Again it was the truth, although Brady knew there was something, a connection between them, that went beyond a casual acquaintance.

"But you go to her place and talk late into the night?"

"I was returning her cookie tin." Even he wasn't buying that one. He knew now he'd been looking for an excuse to see her, spend more time in her serenity. Yet if he hadn't gone there, he would have never ended up asleep on her couch. He would have never been spotted coming out of her back door at dawn. What a mess, and it was his fault.

"That's right." Cooper exchanged glances with the others. "She makes you cookies."

Brady saw his brothers' amused expressions. Jenna came to the screen door again. "Coffee's getting cold, guys."

No one moved.

"Eden makes everybody cookies," Brady argued. "She's a sweet, quiet, good person. A Sunday school teacher type of person. She's not someone people should talk about over morning coffee and Marge's blueberry pancakes. She's a good woman."

Seth looked at Brady and smiled a big brother's smile. "You like her."

"We're friends. No more."

He knew they didn't believe him. The thought of people whispering about Eden and him, the possibility that her reputation had been compromised by his own indiscretion made him sick. He could only hope she hadn't heard any of these untrue accusations. He couldn't allow the whole town to believe she was just another one of Dr. Divine's conquests. He had to do something right now to restore Eden's reputation.

"All right, all right. I'll tell you the truth."

"It's about time," Quinn kidded.

Brady took a deep breath and looked at his family. "I'm the Flower Phantom."

There was silence. Then the smiles around him swelled into laughter.

"And I'm the Tooth Fairy," Seth said.

"You are, Uncle Seth?" Sara charged out the

screen door and stood before her new uncle, awe in her eyes.

"Sara." Molly came to the screen door. "Come on back to the kitchen, honey. It's getting cold out. Daddy and the other men will be right in."

"Mommy?" Sara still looked at Seth with wonder. "Uncle Seth's the Tooth Fairy."

"And Uncle Brady's the Flower Phantom." Quinn smiled.

Sara looked at her new father. "What are you, Daddy?"

He scooped the child up in his arms. He brushed back her bangs and looked into her big blue eyes. "I'm the most wonderful thing of all, darling. I'm a daddy."

"I am the Flower Phantom," Brady insisted. He'd never felt more foolish in his life. It wasn't a comfortable feeling.

Seth laughed. "Brady, if you don't want to talk about your relationship with Eden Frazier, it's okay. The town's doing enough talking, anyway."

"I go to Eden's after hours to order the flowers." His gaze shifted away from the others.

"Do you put on a monkey suit and do gorilla-grams, too?" Quinn wondered.

Brady ignored the men's amused expressions. "One night, on my way home from work, I passed Eden's shop and went inside. On a whim."

"A whim?" Seth was openly incredulous. "This from a man who's never known a spontaneous moment in his life. Stop putting us on, Brady."

"I think it's sweet," Jenna said.

Brady cast her a grateful glance as she came out onto the porch.

"Me, too." Molly followed Jenna. "Why couldn't Brady be the Flower Phantom?"

Seth, Quinn and Coop exchanged helpless glances that said, "Women!"

Jenna put her hands on the expanded width of her hips, spreading her feet apart to balance the awkward shape of her body. "Why couldn't he?" She looked at her husband.

Seth raised his hands. "Okay, I give up. Brady's the Flower Phantom." He still smiled at his brother. "I suppose you want to keep this a family secret, or are you coming out of the closet?"

"Seth," Jenna scolded.

"Honey, I'm sorry, but my brother..." He glanced at Brady. "And he knows I mean this as a compliment. My brother isn't a romantic. He's a pragmatist. It's his sensible nature and cool head that make him such a great surgeon. So, instead of discussing his personal life, if he wants to tell us he's having daffodils delivered all over Tyler, fine." He shot Brady an honest look. "Just don't expect us to believe it."

Brady hadn't expected his family to believe him. His recent behavior was not the Brady they knew: the Brady who organized his life like a Rolodex, who was always cautious, circumspect, fearful he'd do something wrong, make a mistake and someone else he loved would leave him forever. Could he blame them for not believing he might be otherwise, when he himself didn't understand his behavior of late?

Elias had been silent, watching his sons. Now he spoke to all of them. "Let Brady be. The boy can take care of himself. He always has. I don't want to hear any more talk."

The old man's gaze shifted past them. "Let the others talk. You won't stop them, anyway. We'll not add our own fuel to this fire. No more talk, understand? There's been too much talk already. Always too much talk." Elias stood. "End of discussion. It's time for dessert and coffee."

END OF DISCUSSION. That night in the off-white world of his apartment, the words rang in Brady's mind. So many years ago, those words were the answer to everything. Only recently had Brady begun to learn that life wasn't that simple. He wondered if Elias would ever realize it, too.

He went to the kitchen and opened the refrigerator door, even though he wasn't hungry. He shut it, opened the smaller freezer door. He cracked the ice cube trays into the ice container until it was full, then filled each tray with water, lined them up in a row on the empty top shelf. He shut the door, looked around the modern apartment of stark lines and simple furniture that tastefully said success. He went to the teak writing table that he never wrote at and looked out the wide windows to the courtyard swimming pool that he had never swum in. He thought of Eden.

He thought of the things being said, the things he himself had thought. He grew angry. He grew ashamed. He didn't deserve someone like Eden. He didn't deserve anyone. His own mother hadn't wanted him.

Deep down inside him, too deep even for him to know, he'd believed one day Violet would come back or maybe send for him or just once telephone and tell him she loved him.

He wandered the too-large, too-empty room. Now he knew. She would never come back. She was gone. What had happened couldn't be changed. It didn't matter how many illnesses he cured or how many flowers he sent.

But the talk about Eden and himself, the speculative looks, the suggestive smiles, he could change that before any more damage was done to Eden's character.

He wanted to call her, tell her he was sorry, but what if she didn't know about the rumors? He would only cause her pain.

No one else but Eden knew he was the Flower Phantom. His own family had refused to believe it. Why would anyone else? As he'd learned tonight, people would still be skeptical, would only wonder if it was a ploy to protect Eden. The damage to his own professional standing in the medical community would be irreparable.

There was only one other course of action to save

Eden's personal reputation and his professional position. He would have to break off all contact with Eden.

He should go to bed. He'd be in the operating room most of the day tomorrow and needed his rest. He should be able to sleep now. The problem had been solved. He would stop seeing Eden. Her reputation would be salvaged and his image as the dependable, no-nonsense Dr. Spencer would be kept intact. However, his steps were heavy as he headed toward the bedroom. It was as he lay in bed, staring at the ceiling, that his own thoughts from earlier this evening came back to mock him: *Life wasn't that simple.*

He woke with the same heaviness. It stayed with him in the days that followed. Days without Eden. With a discomforting sense of shock, he realized he missed her. He missed her shop with the swirls of color and the smells of home and heaven. He missed her cheery kitchen, her cozy living room where he'd slept too soundly. He even missed the pompous Penelope. And he missed sending the flowers. Sometimes he'd been nearby when the arrangements arrived and had seen firsthand the look of happiness they brought to others. He missed that.

By Friday he decided to call her. Office hours were over and everyone else had gone home to family or friends. He was alone in the office, using the excuse once more of catching up with charts instead of facing his empty apartment and another frozen dinner in a black plastic tray. He picked up the phone, telling himself he wanted to order flowers. Surely one call wouldn't do any harm.

He heard the surprise in Eden's voice when she realized it was him. He listened to her soft voice, imagined her smile. He knew she would never be so forward as to ask why she hadn't heard from him since last Friday night. Still he stressed how busy things had been at the hospital. He wasn't sure if her voice got softer then or if he had only imagined it. All he knew was the sound of it was like a song.

He spoke of the weather. Spring had continued to come in a frenzy of greens and longer, warmer days. People raised their faces to the sun as they walked through the square. Even in the hectic world of the hospital, the new light from the windows washed the mauve walls to amethyst and patients in wheelchairs smiled as they sat outside, dozing in the sun. It was as if some of Eden's world was everywhere now.

And Brady had to wonder if the rumors, like a pestilence, had found their way into The Garden of Eden? He longed to ask her, discuss it with her, tell her how sorry he was, how he hoped she hadn't been hurt by the gossip. But if he brought it up and she didn't know, he would feel even worse.

He had run out of casual conversation. There were too many other important, serious things he wished he could talk to her about. In an act of defiance, he ordered four flower arrangements and three balloon bouquets. They talked for a few minutes more, talk so inconsequential, later he couldn't remember the content. He'd been too busy listening to her voice, imagining her head tipped to the side as she listened to his replies. There was a lull, and he knew if he kept her on the line much longer, it would become awkward. He said goodbye, ending the call. He didn't add he hoped to see her soon. She said goodbye too. She didn't invite him to stop by the shop, and he had to wonder once more if the talk around town had reached her ears and hurt her heart.

After he hung up, he sat at his desk for a long time and did nothing. It was something he rarely did—just sit. There was always something that had to be done and never enough time to do it. There were charts such as those before him now. There were operations to perform, rounds to be made, consultations to be done, journals to read, reports to write. There were always people to heal. There was no time to just sit and stare.

Yet that was what he did. For over an hour Brady sat and stared, thinking nothing except how much he would like to be in Eden's kitchen right now, drinking that horrible herb tea.

Chapter Five

Eden replaced the receiver. The shop had closed several hours ago. Thanks to Christy working extra hours to earn money for her prom dress, all the orders were finished. Yet Eden had still been in the showroom when the phone rang. She'd told herself she was getting ready for the weekend. What she had been doing was waiting for Brady.

She stuck his orders on the board. She went back to the worktable and the swag she was making to decorate the doorway. She unrolled fine wire, gathered the lavender, roses, gypsophila into nosegays and wired them into an overlapping chain. She watched her hands performing the tasks she'd done countless times before; she felt the scratch of dried stems against the pads of her fingers. She knew the tight pull of her ponytail and the slight headache from waiting to eat supper, hoping she'd have someone to invite in and share it with. She could feel every inch of her flesh. Yet, if she looked in the mirror at that moment, she would have been shocked to see a reflection, proof that she did exist.

She had been dismissed.

She bent her head lower, studying the delicate lines, the subtle shades of the flowers before her. Her hands worked quicker, without pause or error. She finished the swag and spread it out across the sales counter. Still her hands didn't pause. She gathered bright pink roses, creamy pink helichrysum, yellow kangaroo paw, oats. She brought out stem wires, tape from the cubbyholes carved into the worktable's legs and formed a circle for a wreath.

As swiftly as she worked, her thoughts spun, examining her relationship with Brady, searching for what had gone wrong. She had enjoyed her time with him. He, too, seemed relaxed and comfortable when they were together. He had come more often, stayed longer, smiled sooner. She had thought they were becoming friends, good friends. Something had happened.

Her hands flew faster, and colors came together and blended like a sudden storm.

The last time she'd seen him had been Friday night. Everything had seemed fine. Now everything was wrong. Something must have happened that night to make Brady decide to keep his distance. She slowed her hands and her hectic thoughts, examining the evening. He'd been tired, even more so than usual. Yet he'd seemed more open, more accessible. She'd shared her paintings with him that night. She remembered how he'd looked at them, looked at her. She'd felt so close to him, closer than friends.

Her hands halted. Her heart dropped. Had he felt it, too, that night—her desire, her longing? She was always so careful, but somehow had she revealed her attraction to him that night? He wouldn't know that long ago she'd realized a relationship between them was inconceivable, even laughable. All he would know was she wanted him.

She searched her memory looking for a clue, something she had done that had exposed her desire. It could have been anything—something she said, a physical gesture, a look, a certain way of smiling. Still she couldn't think of anything she'd done or said that had been different from her usual behavior. If anything, it was everyone else in Tyler who had been acting odd. She thought of Christy's giggles, Annabelle's interrogation, Seth's curious looks, Irene's subtle smile as she said, "I hear he's even starting to make house calls now."

I hear he's even starting to make house calls now. She stepped away from the table frowning.

When Irene made that comment at the bank last Saturday, had she been implying Eden was having an affair with Brady? Could it be possible? Were the suspicions of the townspeople of Tyler not about Brady being the Flower Phantom...but her lover?

It seemed absurd, yet she also knew gossip could be nothing more than one person's assumption spoken aloud to another and then another and another until unproven fiction became indisputable truth.

She thought back again to that morning and Irene's remark. In response, she'd smiled a smile that had become bigger and bigger as if saying yes, it was true, Brady came to her *bed* every night.

Even standing alone in the center of her shop, she colored with embarrassment. The townspeople of Tyler thought she and Brady were having an affair, and she'd unwittingly confirmed it. Brady had heard the talk, knew she hadn't denied it. On the contrary, she'd implied it was true. No wonder he'd stopped calling, stopped coming by. He knew of her attraction to him and was trying to let her down easy.

She wanted to protest she was innocent, but deep inside her, she knew she wasn't innocent. To her dismay, she knew a part of her was actually flattered, the part that had fantasized for so many years that Brady would return her hidden affections. She'd known it would never happen, that her desire for Brady was no more than a harmless dream.

Except her dream had not been harmless. It had destroyed a friendship.

EDEN HESITATED the next morning outside the door to Brady's offices. When she'd told Christy and David she would drop off Tyler General's deliveries, she'd seen Christy's eyebrows lift. David had smiled the knowing smile of a sixteen-year-old. The talk must be all over town by now.

She'd been foolish enough to consider such speculation complimentary. She still found it incredulous. Imagine her, shy, reserved Eden Frazier, considered a femme fatale, a woman of seduction and mystery, entertaining a dark, handsome doctor until dawn? It was so absurd she would've laughed out loud if she hadn't remembered Brady's distant tone last night, his careful choice of words.

A woman passed Eden and went into the offices ahead of her. She followed.

"I'm sorry. Dr. Spencer is covering emergencies this weekend," the receptionist told her. She glanced at her computer screen. "You didn't have an appointment, did you?"

"No, I was just in the building and thought I'd stop in." Eden made her voice breezy.

"If you'd like, I'll let him know you were here, Ms.—?"

Eden paused. "Frazier," she supplied. "Eden Frazier." She saw the receptionist's hand go still on the message pad. The swivel of the nurse's head at the filing cabinet was less indiscreet.

"Any other message, Ms. Frazier?" The receptionist waited, pen poised. The nurse's attention returned to the cabinet's opened drawer, but she didn't resume rifling through the files. For a mad moment, Eden had an urge to say something shocking that would spread through the hospital quicker than a microorganism.

What was happening to her? She was here to save her friendship with Brady, not to destroy the dull Goody Two-shoes image the whole town had of her—no matter how intriguing the idea might be.

"No," she said in a polite, most Eden-like tone.

"I'll contact him at a time that's more convenient for him." She saw the nurse at the filing cabinet smile. It was the same smile she'd seen on David this morning.

Coffee, she thought as she came out of the office into the hall. In her hurry to get ahead in the shop so she could run the deliveries over here this morning, she hadn't even taken time for a cup of tea. But she didn't want tea. She wanted coffee, hot, strong and sweet with cream and three sugars.

She took the elevator to the ground floor and followed the arrows pointing the way to the main building. She came to the waiting room with the vinyl couches and chairs and the walls a color that should have been put out of its misery a long time ago. The coffee shop was next to the gift shop. It wasn't until she saw the sign Outpatient and Emergency that she realized she'd made a wrong turn somewhere. She turned to retrace her steps and saw through the secured glass doors of the Emergency Room, Brady talking to Dr. Baron. He wore green scrubs. A matching cap concealed his dark-brown hair, and a mask still loosely tied around his neck rested on his chest. His brow was set in the frown she'd seen so often whenever he concentrated.

It had only been a week since she'd last seen him. To her heart, it seemed forever. The boldness that had brought her here vanished. She turned to go. She had passed the triage desk and was in the hall when she heard him call her name.

She stopped. She should smile, she thought as she

turned, but she couldn't. He wasn't smiling either as he headed toward her, his step always sure. On the contrary, his frown deepened. This was a mistake. She shouldn't have come. She could have sent him a letter but knew it was the action of a coward, its impersonalness an insult. She could have called but feared, unless face-to-face, she'd never have the courage to say the words that needed to be said.

She didn't step toward him, only waited like a trapped animal until he reached her.

"Eden." He pronounced her name precisely. His voice would never be breathless. "What are you doing here?"

She looked up into the green earth of his eyes and forgot the speech she'd practiced for the past sleepless hours.

He ran his hand across his crown, pulling off the surgical cap and crinkling it in his fist. "Why didn't you let me know you were coming? What if I wasn't here?" His voice was stern. "Never mind." He took her arm, leading her back to Emergency. "I am here and I'll make sure you have the best care possible."

She stopped in the middle of the hall, understanding. A smile came to her face, and her insides turned warm. "Brady." She put her hand on his, wrapped around her arm. "I'm not sick."

He looked at her. How had she forgotten how tall he always seemed, although he was normal height for a man? She saw relief flash across his face before his features once more became calm and in charge.

"I had some deliveries," she explained.

"Of course." He released her arm.

"But I did stop by your office."

"And they told you I was here?" He took her elbow once more, moving her closer to the wall to let a gurney pass. Brady nodded to the orderly.

"Actually, I was going to get a cup of coffee on my way out, but I got turned around somehow and ended up here by accident."

He half smiled. "I don't believe in accidents."

She took a deep breath. "Hopefully, you don't believe in rumors, either."

His green eyes met hers. His face was unreadable. A group passed, many in scrubs similar to Brady's. A man in a white starched coat, a stethoscope looped around his neck, said hello. Brady nodded again, but his gaze stayed on Eden.

"Generally I prefer fact over innuendo." He touched her hand as if she were a patient. "But sometimes the line blurs, and before you know it, innuendo is being accepted for fact. And people get hurt."

Eden looked up into his eyes. The constant press of people and machines moving through the hall had forced them closer. She could see the bare beat of pulse in his throat. She saw the man who sent flowers to the sick and the sad; the man who was, after all, only human. "And good friendships end unnecessarily."

An orderly pushing a patient in a wheelchair nodded to Brady. Brady looked around. "Perhaps we should talk somewhere less..."

"Public?" she supplied.

The thin smile returned. He took her elbow and led her again toward Emergency. He pressed a sequence of buttons on the lock outside the double glass doors and they swung open to a hall lined with machines and empty stretchers. He ushered her past the high counter of the nurses' station, the rows of narrow curtained areas, a cart filled with linens. He stopped before an opened door, waved her inside and followed her, snapping on the overhead light as he shut the door.

There was the artificial odor of trapped air. Tall metal racks surrounded them, leaving only a narrow square of space within the compact room. Eden and Brady backed away until their spines hit the wire shelves filled with sterile gloves, IV solutions, catheter kits and other medical supplies. Still they were too close.

Eden felt her muscles constrict, her body trying to take up less space. Brady cleared his throat, the sound too loud in the cramped space. They'd been alone before. They'd always been alone. Never had they been so aware of it, so uncomfortable. The tension was tangible. It was all her fault.

"Brady, I'm so sorry."

The surprise on his face was the last reaction she expected.

"You're sorry? No, Eden." He reached as if to touch her hand. She knew it was a learned gesture. His hand hesitated, dropped to his side. He was no longer the doctor; she was no longer the patient.

"I'm the one who should be apologizing. All week I've wanted to talk to you about this whole situation, but I didn't know if you'd heard the rumors."

The hand that had reached for her massaged his brow. "But of course you have. This is Tyler. I should've remembered that. I should've remembered how easily rumors get started before I began making late-night stops at your shop." He shook his head at his own stupidity. "I should've remembered all those things before I ruined your reputation."

So, she'd been right. Irene and the others didn't think Brady was the Flower Phantom. They thought he was her lover. And what had she'd done? Met every innuendo with a big smile on her face, satisfying their every suspicion.

"Actually, I was worried about your reputation," she told him.

"My reputation? Dr. Meet-and-Mate?" He rolled his eyes. "I know all about it. Damn gossip."

"Dr. Meet-and-Mate?" Now she was getting confused. "No, I was worried the townspeople suspected you were the Flower Phantom."

He released a self-righteous snort. "My own family laughed when I told them the truth. That's when I decided people are going to believe what they want to. Staying away from the shop seemed like the best solution. I'm afraid it's too little, too late. The damage has been done. I'm sorry, Eden. I never meant to put you in this sort of…compromising situation."

She stared at him, starting to understand. "That's

why you've stayed away from the shop? To stop the talk? You were worried about my reputation.''

''Of course. Why else would I have stopped coming?''

''I thought...'' She looked into his eyes, emerald in the overhead light. ''I thought I might have done something, said something that...upset you.''

''Like what?''

She hesitated. If she told him the real reason why she'd thought he'd stopped coming—that he'd sensed her attraction to him—the awkwardness between them would only worsen instead of be resolved.

''Eden,'' he said as she tried to form an answer, ''you were the one who always stayed open late for me, made me cookies, lent me your sofa. What could you ever do to upset me?''

She shifted her weight. She had to tell him. She couldn't let him take the whole blame. ''When I went to the bank last Saturday morning, Irene Smythe made an odd comment about you making house calls. I thought she was hinting that she knew you were the Flower Phantom, so I just smiled, pretending not to understand what she was talking about. Then I realized she might think you were making late-night visits for another...'' Eden searched for the right word. ''More risqué reason. You can imagine how silly that seemed and, well...'' Eden shifted from one foot to the other. ''I might've smiled wider. I'm afraid Irene mistook that smile for a sign that said you and I were having an affair.''

Brady shook his head. "I was the one Herb Smythe saw coming out of your building at dawn last Saturday morning. I was the one Anna Kelsey and Martha Bauer saw leaving your place by the back alley. All this talk about you and me—it's my fault."

"It's not your fault."

"Well, it's not yours."

She might have smiled if not for the stricken expression on Brady's face.

He rubbed his brow. "I hope the whole situation didn't upset you too much."

"Upset me? I'm going to enjoy every minute of it."

"Enjoy it?"

"I'm going to sit in my shop and enjoy every second of my notoriety." Now she did smile. "It's not every day a person, never mind a whole town, thinks of me as a sexpot."

Still the ever-present lines on his forehead only pulled together as he studied her. "You're an attractive woman, Eden," he diagnosed.

Gosh, she had missed her friend. "And you're sweeter than Britt Marshack's pastries." She put her palm to his cheek. Just as quickly she took it away.

"And if you want to come by the shop, come." She broke the sudden silence. "Whenever you want to."

He looked at her, still contrite.

"Please?" she added.

"That's nice of you, Eden, but people will talk."

"Let them talk. I'd rather have a friend than a sterling reputation anyday." She gave him a conspirator's smile. "Actually, I've been trying to get rid of that reputation for years. Good riddance."

He looked at her, unconvinced.

"Please come by the shop. You're welcome anytime."

He shook his head. "I don't want you to get hurt."

She was going to lose him. "I missed you, Brady." The words were out of her mouth before she realized she was going to say them. They hung in the odd-smelling air. She couldn't meet his eyes.

"I missed you, too, Eden."

Now the air seemed thick, heavy, as if its invisible touch could be felt. It was too close.

"I missed your cookies," he said.

When she raised her head to find him watching her, she smiled. Finally he did, too. The air became light again, allowing normal breath.

"Friends?" she asked.

"Friends." He held out his hand. It was such a strong, capable hand, the fingers broad, the nails clipped neat. She put her own small one next to it, felt the dry touch of his palm, the wistful wanting always inside her.

There were steps outside the door. The knob twisted right and left. A female voice said, "Who locked the door to the supply room?" Eden and

Brady didn't breathe. "Left the damn light on, too. Now I've got to go get a key. Like I don't have enough to do. Three short, and Saturday night coming up."

Brady looked at Eden as they listened to the muttering retreat. "The door must've automatically locked when it closed."

She nodded. "I should get back to the shop. I left Christy all alone."

"And I'm on call." He looked at her hand in his, but he didn't let go. Instead his fingers tightened as he bowed his head to give her a kiss on the cheek. It was a brush of lips, a kiss between friends, but still it was enough to make Eden's face flush. He opened the door and snapped the light off as they went into the hall. She could still feel the heat in her cheeks.

They saw the nurses and techs gape at them, their gazes follow them as they passed the nurses' station. Brady pressed a button on the wall and the double doors swung open.

"I think I can find my way back now," Eden told him as he walked with her into the half-full waiting area. "You must have work to do."

"I always have work to do, but how often do I get to walk with a friend?" He winked as if to say, "Let 'em talk." She'd never seen him wink before.

She smiled as they walked together. At the main doors, he offered his hand once more. "Friends," he said.

"You'll come by the shop whenever you want?"

"Neither wild horses nor wicked tongues could keep me away."

She placed her palm to his. "Friends."

She went out the wide doors into the day's clear light, but she turned as if knowing he'd still be standing there. He was. She waved and then continued toward the flower shop. Smiling the whole way.

BRADY WAS SMILING, TOO, as he walked up Maple Street toward his childhood home. The big Victorian, the color of storm clouds and trimmed with gray, still stood sober and staid, dominating the block like an old schoolmaster. The house should really be painted, Brady thought, and join its less-impressive but more-colorful and cheerful neighbors. As long as he remembered, the house had worn its hair shirt of solemn colors. So had its inhabitants.

He neared the wide steps to the porch, the sounds of voices and laughter from inside already reaching him. At the screen door he was welcomed by the smells of Eva's roast cooking and pies cooling. This was how it should've always been, he thought. This was how it might have been if his mother had stayed. He pushed the thought from his mind before the emotions came. He thought of Eden and her homey apartment.

He followed the voices to the large, old-fashioned kitchen where everybody always seemed to gather. Through the row of windows that looked out to the backyard, he saw Elias on his knees in one of the beds, pulling at a tangle of dried stalks, reaching beneath the winter cover of dead leaves, bringing up a handful of soil he let sift through his fingers. Quinn was prancing around the perimeter of the yard, Sara on his shoulders.

"What's the old man doing?" Brady asked.

"Says he's gardening." Seth came and stood beside him.

"C'mon. His idea of gardening is to slip the boy who does the lawn for the summer a few extra dollars to pull a few weeds or whack off some of that shabby stuff once in a while."

"Says he's gardening," Seth repeated, watching his father.

"Well, he can't do any harm. The beds can't look any worse than they do. He let them go too long."

"They didn't always look like that."

Brady glanced at his brother. Seth's gaze was steady on their father.

Brady looked again to the yard. "I don't know why he doesn't just hire a professional service to come in and clean them up."

Seth turned to him. "It was Mom's garden. She planted it that first summer."

Brady looked away from his father and the neglected garden. Quinn was lying on the new grass, his knees pulled up to his chest. Sara, standing above him, leaned forward, her body stiff, her stomach meeting the raised soles of his feet. She joined her hands with his, her face filling with joy as Quinn slowly stretched his legs, lifting her up, up, her body balanced and straight, her arms stretched out like wings, her hands tight in his. Brady watched the man and child. Like a picture, he saw Quinn above him, arms spread wide as he balanced on the soles of Brady's feet, his brother's face turned toward the sky and so taken with wonder, he might really have been flying. The memory had been jogged and now held fast. It was a moment from a long time ago, the time before his mother had left them.

As he turned from the window, he saw Seth watching Quinn and Sara, too.

"We used to do that." Seth looked at him. "Remember me giving you an airplane ride like that when you were a little punk?"

Brady shook his head. He didn't want to remember himself so innocent that being lifted three feet off the ground made him believe he was flying. His life was divided into two periods—before his mother left and afterward. He never thought about the former and rarely examined the latter. He preferred to stay in the here-and-now where memories couldn't come and feelings weren't acknowledged.

Seth tried again. "How 'bout the time I shot a BB into your butt?"

"Seth!" Jenna protested from the table where she and Molly were looking at a baby furniture catalog.

"Hey, that's what got him into surgery. He has me to thank for what he is today."

"The only thing I have to thank you for today is the scar on my left cheek," Brady told him.

"So, tell the chicks it's a war wound. They dig

that kind of thing, don't they, girls?'' Seth looked at his wife and sister-in-law.

Molly looked at Jenna. "Girls?"

Jenna looked at Molly. "Chicks?" She spoke to the expanded curve of her belly. "Sorry you had to hear that."

Quinn came in with Sara thrown over his shoulder, squirming and giggling. "Oh, boy, what did Uncle Seth do now, Sara?" he said, swinging the child upside down, summoning more shrieks and giggles.

"I was just asking these wonderful representatives of the female race—" Seth glanced at his wife and Jenna nodded her approval "—if it's the BB scar on Brady's butt that makes all the ladies swoon."

"I always thought it was the main source of his charm," Quinn said, swinging Sara upright and propping her on his hip. "Maybe we should ask Eden."

There was only the sound of Sara's humming as she rested her head on Seth's shoulder.

"Seth!" Now it was Molly's turn to scold her husband.

Brady's good mood vanished. "This topic was resolved at last week's family dinner," he said stiffly.

Quinn looked at Seth. "I can see why you used to shoot him in the butt."

"Listen," Brady said, "I told you exactly a week ago today, there is nothing going on between Eden

Frazier and me. I thought we were clear on this matter.''

"Well, little brother, we were." Seth looked at Quinn and winked. "Until we heard you took Eden Frazier into a hospital supply closet. And it wasn't to do inventory."

"Actually that's the G-rated version," Quinn noted. "They say the version going round the farm and machinery plant would make even Tisha Olsen blush. I don't know, Brady. Don't you think it's time you made an honest woman out of Eden?"

Seth shook his head. "I'm beginning to think he's afraid to bring Eden around us." He looked at Quinn. "You think he's ashamed of us?"

"Could be." Quinn played along. "He'll do anything to avoid introducing us to Ms. Frazier. Even swear he's the Flower Phantom."

"Can you blame him?" Molly sent Brady a sympathetic look.

"He has gone to great lengths to keep this relationship a secret." Seth agreed with Quinn. "Trying to make us believe he was just scoping out Eden for her snapdragons."

"Don't pay them any mind, Brady." Jenna tried to console him.

"Hey, Brady, why don't I go up in the attic right now and look for that BB gun?" Molly offered. "I'll let you have the first shot."

Brady said nothing. He stared out the windows, past his father crouched in the garden to the black and green and brown of the farm fields beyond. A heaviness pulled on his features, weighted his body.

"Tell Dad I'm sorry, but I can't stay for Sunday dinner tonight." Without looking at any of them, he turned and walked out.

"Now you see what you guys did?" he heard Jenna say.

As he crossed to the front door, it opened and Coop came in. "Emergency call?" Coop asked, but Brady only hurried past him and down the porch steps.

Coop went into the kitchen. "What's wrong with the doc?"

Seth looked at Quinn and both turned toward the women that had become their wives and the center of their worlds. "Nothing that can't be cured."

THE GARDEN OF EDEN'S back door was always unlocked when Brady came. The door to Eden's apartment was also open, left ajar several inches as if she'd been listening for someone. Past the open door he heard music, the light sounds contrasting with his heavy steps up the stairs.

"Brady."

For the first time since he'd left his father's house, Brady stopped.

Eden stood at the top of the stairs, surprise and delight on her face. She wore a long, too-big skirt and a cropped, sleeveless T-shirt, its neckband circling her throat. She was shoeless. Her light-blue socks bagged around her ankles.

He wanted to kiss her. Not a friendly hello on the cheek but a real kiss—long, deep, slow, a delicate sweep of his tongue as he took her, her slender body meeting his, the taste of her sweet inside him. He wanted to discover the body that hinted at more than fragile ankles and shockingly sweet knees. He wanted to hold her, kiss her, feel her breasts full and warm in his cupped hands, feel his body buried deep inside her, moving with her, within her. Wanting slammed into him as hard as when he'd heard his brothers joke that he'd had sex with Eden in the supply closet.

He heard his labored breaths and blamed them on running all the way here.

"This is a nice surprise." It was the sparkle in her eyes that told him she'd been waiting, hoping he'd come.

Those eyes that made him want to lose himself. "I thought you had dinner with your family on Sunday nights?" That voice that made his heart beat faster.

She knew so many things about him, things he'd shared with no one else. He looked up into those clear, crazy-colored eyes and wondered how deep did they see? Did they see the wild desire building inside him as if the rumors were true? Did they see that he'd come here, run all the way, to tell her they couldn't see each other anymore?

Chapter Six

Brady climbed the last two steps and went into the kitchen. Eden already had the kettle on.

"Wasn't it a lovely day?" She moved about the kitchen, gathering an extra cup and spoon, the sugar bowl, the plastic bear of honey. "After church I went for a long walk out past the plant toward the lake. Then I sat all afternoon in the square and read the Sunday *Tyler Citizen*. Gosh, it was a gorgeous day."

She glanced at him as she put a plate of cookies on the table. He was still standing in the doorway and had said nothing.

"Of course, I made sure I wore my scarlet letter everywhere I went."

He half smiled. The kettle began to steam.

"Come in, come in." She gestured at the table. "Sit down. Your timing is perfect. I was just making some tea." She went to the stove and took the kettle off the burner. "I'm afraid I'm out of everything but cinnamon spice."

"That's fine."

She shook two tea bags out of a box. "Sit down," she told him once more. Her voice was still gay, but concern had come into her eyes.

He walked in, pulled out a chair and sat. As he looked around, the unease swelled within him. Past the doorway into the living room, there was a half-finished painting propped on an easel. The shiny light and dark of its colors indicated it was still drying.

She saw him looking at the piece as she carried the cups to the table and sat down across from him. "Next people will be saying I lured you up here to 'see my etchings.'" Her smile was too big, too desperate. She sensed something was wrong.

He finally spoke. "It wouldn't be any worse than what they're saying now."

She dunked her tea bag up and down, pressed it against the spoon's bowl, squeezing it dry. She glanced at him, but her gaze dropped to his cup of tea. "You shouldn't let it get too strong."

"They say the latest rumors going around are enough to make Tisha Olsen blush," he said.

She reached over and slid his cup toward her, fished the tea bag out.

"I told you I don't care about all that." She wrapped the tag's string around the tea bag, squeezed it against the spoon. "I don't care what everybody says." She slid the cup back and looked at him. He saw shades of wild iris in her eyes.

"They're saying we had sex in the supply closet when you came to the hospital yesterday."

She stared at him, the lines of her face delicate and her eyes seeming even larger, richer in color. Her hands daintily held the thick mug. "They said we had sex in the supply closet?"

He nodded, watching her, worried.

She looked down into the mug, contemplating her tea, then set the cup down and pushed away from the table. Wrapping a napkin around the used tea bags, she walked to the sink and opened the cupboard beneath it. She threw the tea bags into the wastebasket. "They said we were having sex in the hospital supply closet yesterday...."

She closed the cupboard door and straightened. Still with her back to him, she looked out the window with its cheery yellow-and-blue curtains. Then he saw her shoulders shake, and he was on his feet and at her side.

"Eden, I'm so sorry about all of this." He placed his hands on her trembling shoulders. "I never meant for you to get hurt." He heard light bubbles of breath being released. "Eden, I'll make sure this—" The breaths came quicker; her whole body shook. "Eden, are you okay?"

The shallow breaths broke into delicate giggles.

"Eden?" He turned her toward him. Her lips were pressed tight, trying to hold her amusement in, but her body shook until her laughter escaped and rippled in the air. "Are you okay?"

Her eyes were gem bright, her lips in a lovely

curve. She caught her breath and patted his hands, still holding her shoulders. "I'm fine, Doctor. I'm fine."

He studied her. "And this—you and me in the supply room—this is funny?"

Her head tipped back, and he heard her soft laughter once more. He frowned.

She wiped at her eyes. "I'm sorry. It's just the thought of me and you…in a supply closet, no less." She shook her head, and new laughter came. "You've got to admit it's funny."

He smiled uncertainly. His hands let go of her and returned to his sides.

She went to the table, picked up her tea and took a sip. "I mean who would ever believe you were so hot for me, you seduced me in a supply closet?"

"Obviously the town of Tyler."

"It's ridiculous."

"Less than thirty minutes ago my brothers were demanding that I make a decent woman out of you."

She was laughing again.

He frowned. "I'm not so sure it's that funny, Eden."

"Oh, God, it is. It is." She set down her tea and stepped back from the table. "Look at me." She pressed her lips together again, trying not to giggle. "Just look at me."

He began at the top. Her hair fell straight and free today. It had brushed his knuckles when he'd held her, its touch light and soft as wings. Her eyes were bold, too bright, too beautiful in her colorless face; her smile was warm and always gentle. Her clothes were long and loose except for the T-shirt's tight circle around her neck. Her body was covered but the bared, unbroken line of her arms took his breath away.

Her narrow shoulders lifted. "Do you see before you a woman whom single, sexy surgeons ravish in supply closets?"

Sexy. For a moment, he didn't know what to say. Then he did. "Sexy?"

She laughed lightly. "You have your reputation..." She turned from him, taking away the bold color of her eyes, the easy smile curving her lips. "I have mine."

When she turned back, her smile was smaller. She patted the table. "Your tea is getting cold."

He didn't move. "If I hadn't been so damn worried about my reputation, yours would be intact."

She looked at him. "Believe me, no one is more intact than I."

He shook his head. "This is my fault—all this talk going around town. I should've thought before I came here, before I sent the flowers."

"Don't you dare apologize, Brady Spencer."

The uncustomary sternness in her voice stopped him.

"What you did—sending those flowers, giving gifts, giving people what they needed when they needed it most, all without obligation or for any other reason than to make someone happy—it was beautiful. I'm proud to have had a small part in it.''

Her voice was fierce. Her eyes flashed. He had never seen her like this and could only look at her. She shifted her weight and folded her arms across her waist as if suddenly self-conscious.

''So let them talk.'' Her voice was soft again. She looked away from him and patted the table once more. ''Drink your tea.''

Her gaze was averted, her arms wrapped tight to her chest. He saw the way she tried to hide her body, hide herself. He saw the girl who'd been laughed at when she fell. He saw the girl made invisible by a too-big, too-noisy world. And so, she had made her own world, a world she'd shared with him. A world where he'd been happy.

He looked at Eden and knew she had no idea how really beautiful she was. He stepped toward her and touched her shoulder. She started. Those huge eyes stared up at him. His hand smoothed across her collarbone, pushed back her hair from the side of her face. He bowed his head and kissed the jawline he'd uncovered. The fingertips of his other hand touched her cheek, the cheek he had kissed yesterday, the soft, soft skin. Her eyes watched him, anxious, fearful.

''Are you afraid?'' he murmured against her flesh.

She shook her head no, then nodded yes.

He smiled, kissing each wide eye closed. His lips traced a curve to her ear, and he whispered, ''Me, too.'' For the first time in his life.

Her lower lip trembled. He moved his mouth toward hers—just a light kiss, a healing kiss, a kiss to take away the tremble. His mouth met her lips, nipped the bottom one, sucked it gently, her lip soft and wet. He tasted no tremble. Instead he felt it beneath his hands, wherever he touched. He kissed the bottom lip, now still, the top lip, each corner. It was not enough.

He felt a warmth on his chest. Eden was touching him, the tremble there in her fine-wristed white hands.

He bowed his head as if to say a prayer, and his mouth, still soft and moist but hungry now, opened, covering hers. He heard a low sound of surprise from the back of her throat; her lips, pinched at the corners, went lax, and the sound came again. Still it was not enough.

His fingers weaved through her hair, his hands angling her head, tilting her mouth to his. His tongue teased her lips, venturing slightly where the lips had parted. His tongue withdrew, returned, its motion like a pulse beat now. He tasted the tremble once more.

This is Eden. The thought was a delirium. *Eden, Eden, Eden.* He eased back, searching for sanity. There was only a breath between the wet softness of their mouths. When had he begun to shake? He leaned back several inches now, his hands finding the semineutral area of her shoulders, steadying her, himself. He looked down, saw her white hands splayed against his shirt, the heaving rise and fall of his chest. "Eden, I'm sorry."

He took another step back. Her hands tightened on his chest, gathered his shirt in her fists and held fast.

Eyes like a sunrise looked up at him. "Eden, I just—"

She stood on her toes. The tip of her tongue gingerly touched the curve of his mouth, and his words were swallowed, his reason stolen. He pulled her to him, all gentleness gone, her lips already parting, the pink tip of her tongue coming forward. He caught her mouth with his. There was a gasp, the sweet intake of breath, and he was inside her, the wet walls of her mouth contracting as her breath caught.

His fingers slipped beneath the tight neck of her shirt to circle her throat, his thumb stroking the pulse beating at the base of her neck, while his tongue circled inside her, prodding, dancing. He licked the roof of her mouth. The taste of her was cinnamon and rich and slick.

Her hand holding fast to his shirt knotted, wrenching the cloth away from his skin as her body curved toward him and her head fell back, drinking him deeper inside her.

Longing took him hard as the tiny hand clenched against his chest. He ran his hands down her back, feeling the thin, tight muscles there, the bony rope of the spine. Her body was warm against him and tinier than he thought. He wrapped his arms around her, wanting her near him, wanting to cover her completely, suddenly feeling large and clumsy against her. Her skin, her hair, everywhere, smelled of spring. It was her magic. This was Eden.

He pulled back gently, taking his mouth away slowly, brushing his lips against hers, trailing moist kisses across her cheek to the wing of her eyebrow. He saw her eyes still closed, her lips opened. She panted silently. His lips moved to her throat where the flesh was even warmer, its scent fuller. He heard her gasp as he pressed his open mouth to her neck, tasting that fertile flesh. He buried his face against the life that beat there and breathed in the scent of rain. He burrowed deeper into the warmth, the pulse, the perfumed flesh.

He had to go now.

Or he would never leave.

He raised his head. Her eyes opened, bright and wondering. He stepped back, his own body clenching when he saw her eyes question, the colors cloud.

"Eden, I don't know—" He could still feel the heat of her body. He took another step back, absently touching the wrinkled, damp spot on his shirt where her hand had held him.

"Brady?" Her voice shook. Her body braced. She was only learning this game between a man and woman. "I want this." She touched her throat where he had last tasted her. The taste was still sweet in his mouth. "If you do." The tremble came again. In her. In him.

He took her in his arms before he could think, before he could list all the reasons why he should say good-night. He felt the hard tips of her nipples, the thrust of his thigh between hers, her hands fluttering across his back as if not certain where to go. This was Eden.

He raised his head once more. Her eyes opened, questioning, worried. He curved his hands around her wondering face, kissed her lips again and again until her eyelids fluttered closed once more.

"Slow, Eden," he murmured, his breath fanning her cheek. "I'll go slow. We'll go slow." His lips glided across the silk of her skin. "Okay?"

She nodded, her eyes staying closed, her hands clutching his shoulders as if he would go. He released her face and it turned to press against his. His hands slid down the curves of her, rested on her hips and waited. He pressed against her lightly, and when her legs spread, he allowed his hands to circle her hips, her buttocks, knowing his restraint wouldn't last long.

"Take me into your bedroom," he whispered. He waited for her to open her eyes and look into his. There was still time to say no, his gaze told her.

She took his hand, raised it to her lips and kissed it, then led him into her bedroom.

The darkness had only just come. She went to the windows and pulled closed the sheer curtains, painting the room with a rosy tone. She turned to look at him and smiled uncertainly, then walked to the canopy bed with the garlands of flowers wound around its poles and the richly colored canvases hidden beneath it.

She sat, gathering the hem of her short T-shirt in her hands and pulling it over her head until his hands caught hers. He kneeled in front of her and allowed his own hands to finish what she had begun. Then she was before him, the white lace edge of her bra cut low across the pale curves of her breasts. She sat so very still, those wild-violet eyes staring into his, her arms stiff, her palms pressed to the white lace of the bedcovers. His face near to hers, he slipped the straps slowly down her shoulders until they lay loose against her arms. As he slid his fingers to the white lace edge of her bra, he felt her skin rise up in shivers. He bowed his head to taste the flesh, even sweeter there. He heard the intake of breath above him, felt his resistance weaken. His fingers found the clasp and, undoing it, he pushed away the virginal cotton, his fingers slipping beneath to the soft, heated spill of flesh and the hard, teasing tips.

He leaned forward into heat and softness and damp skin. His lips grazed a breast tinted rose, nuzzling, mouthing flesh, finding the tight bud painted a deeper rose and drawing it deep inside the warmth of his mouth.

He heard her whisper his name, felt her hands thread through his hair and pull him tightly to her, her chest rising and falling unevenly as he suckled her. He found the other breast, his lips nuzzling its rose curves, his tongue flicking across its taut nipple. Taking it into the moist circle of his mouth, he suckled and tongued and licked, losing himself in the smoothness and sweetness of her, her heat all around him, his own heat inside him.

He tore his mouth away from her, moving up the base of her throat, wanting to see her eyes bright in the rose-colored light. His hands covered her breasts, the thick skin of his palms moving back and forth across the tight tips, the friction of flesh on flesh.

He found her mouth first and, taking it, drew her tongue forward, drawing it inside him, pulling it deeper and deeper, until it tasted him, stroked him, until she took his own breath for hers.

He pulled his mouth away and, leaning his forehead on hers, saw her eyes overbright. "Eden?" His fingertip touched a damp streak on her cheek. His tongue touched the spot and tasted salt.

"Eden?" His fingertip touched her cheek once more and caught a tear.

She pulled back from his touch. Her hand impatiently brushed away the tear and the next one, too. Still they came, silently sliding down her skin. She smiled, and he could see the woman and the girl both within her. "It's just that... I never knew... I've never..."

She was silent, but her wet face, only inches away from his, said it all.

Never? Brady sat back on his haunches. *Never?* Surely there'd been boyfriends, steadies? Someone she'd thought she loved and a night when there was a pale moon she would always remember and a moment that would never come again. No one goes twenty-seven years without falling senselessly in love with someone. Eden was a good girl, but even good girls did it.

She saw his face. "Don't stop. I don't want you to stop."

"Eden." His hands, hands that had touched her intimately, now fisted atop his thighs. He closed his eyes, dropped his head on her knee and let go a shuddering breath. Her hands tentatively touched his head, hands that had moments ago twined in his hair, pressed him close to her.

What had he done?

He was a man. She was a woman. He wanted her. She wanted him. It seemed simple. Except sex was never simple. Even between experienced partners, it was treacherous. Seducing a virgin was equal to walking through a minefield.

He raised his head, looked at Eden naked and vulnerable above him. He raised himself up on his knees and took both her hands in his. She bit her lower lip.

"Eden—"

She pulled her hands away. "I'm not a patient, Brady. I didn't bring you in here for a diagnosis."

He didn't know what to say. He dropped back once more and looked at her.

She looked away. "I'm a woman." Her gaze moved back to him. "I'm a woman. I know what I want. I told you what I want." Her arms folded across her nakedness.

"This isn't what you want, Eden." His hand instinctively reached to touch her, soothe her. He felt for this woman more than he could express to her. To himself. The last thing in the world he wanted was to hurt her.

He wanted her to be happy. He wanted her to have everything she deserved, everything he knew she dreamed of—a home, a family, a man who loved her and would make her happy for the rest of her life.

He wasn't that man.

She eyed his hand and it halted midair. Her gaze stayed on it until it dropped back to his knee.

"You know what I want?" She quietly challenged him.

"Yes." Their gazes met. "And it's something I can't give—"

She shook her head, cutting him off. She knew what he would say. She even knew he was right. Still she didn't want to hear it.

"I want...I want..." She couldn't look at him anymore. She looked away, seeing the rocking chair with the needlepoint cushions and the Raggedy Ann and Andy dolls propped on its seat, their hands crossed. She wiggled into her bra and sighed. "I want to stop being the oldest twenty-seven-year-old virgin in America."

"One day, Eden, the right guy is going to come along, and you'll have all the happiness you deserve."

She looked him in the eye. "Please don't patronize me."

He rose to a crouching position and placed his hands on her shoulders before she could stop him. "Any man would consider himself lucky to have you."

She felt his skin on her skin and was too conscious of her own half-dressed state. "You've been listening to too many rumors, Doc."

"Wait, Eden. Wait for that right guy."

She had. She'd waited since she was eight.

She bent and reached for her T-shirt, sliding out from his grasp. If she made light of the situation, maybe she'd get through this with a little of her dignity left. She pulled the T-shirt over her head. "Just my luck. I pick a Casanova with a conscience."

Brady smiled as he stood. "Friends?" She saw his hand start to reach for hers, then stop and return to his side.

"Always," she said. She wanted to touch him, too, to reassure him nothing had changed, but she didn't dare. With a twist of her heart, she realized, everything had changed.

"I should go," he said. He nodded as if seconding his decision. "Monday morning and all that, you know."

The awkwardness had already started.

She smoothed her shirt, ran her hand across the nape of her neck where damp hair stuck. They went into the living room. Penelope, stretched out on the couch, raised her head as they came into the room and eyed the couple.

"Busy week ahead?" Eden asked to fill the silence. She who had always felt most comfortable in the quiet suddenly needed noise, voices, sound, anything to override the thoughts circling inside her head.

"Busy week ahead," Brady confirmed. "I doubt I'll be doing much of anything but working."

She'd make it easy for him. "So I probably won't be seeing much of you?"

"Probably not."

She missed a step even though she knew his answer before he spoke. She corrected her pace before he noticed.

"It's probably for the best, though, with all this talk going around. In fact, that was why I came over tonight—to suggest we see a little less of each other in the hope that this nonsense dies down."

Her heart shrank. She'd mistaken pity for passion.

"I know you say you don't care what people think, but, Eden, I won't have these rumors going around about you. It's unfair to you. Sex in the supply room, for God's sake."

A frown lined his forehead. Light laughter concealed the emotion inside her. "It's funny, isn't it? First we don't see each other because I'm supposedly not a virgin. Now we won't see each other because I am a virgin." She heard the edgy amusement in her voice. "Damned if I do and damned if I don't." She looked away. All her dignity was lost.

"Eden."

She didn't look at him. She didn't want to see his professional expression of concern.

"Eden, I don't want to see you hurt—not by other people...not by me."

She heard the caring in his voice, knew how he hated to see anyone in pain. It was his avowed oath: First do no harm.

"I would never make a promise to you I couldn't keep."

She heard the truth, the truth she had always known but had somehow forgotten in these past few weeks. Even still, it hurt. Head turned, she closed her eyes, knowing she had no one to blame but herself. And her foolish hopes.

"You've waited, Eden, waited a long time, and do you know why?"

She opened her eyes, forced her features into a dignified mask. It was the least she could do for him, for herself.

"Because you're not a one-night-stand type of woman."

She managed a smile. Noble, honorable Brady. He was a good man. Even if he didn't know it.

"You're the type of woman who gives her whole heart to one man. The right man. That's what you're waiting for. The right man."

"You're right." She gave him a smile, letting him leave. She closed the door after him, listened to his descending steps. He was right. All these years, she had been waiting for the right man. That one special man who would love her the morning after and the morning after that and all the mornings of her life.

But, in the meantime, she'd fallen in love with Brady Spencer.

Chapter Seven

"Nails," Nadine said.

"Excuse me?" Eden asked, not looking up from the dish garden she was creating. The new stylist at The Hair Affair often spent her lunch hour at the flower shop, visiting with Eden. In a brief period the two women had become good friends. Eden heard the scrape of the wrought iron chair. Seconds later, a set of vixen-length, gold-frosted nails with a black diagonal stripe across each one waved beneath her nose. Eden looked up into the blue eyes of the other woman.

"Nails," Nadine pronounced once more.

Eden had already learned Nadine never made a point without dramatics if possible. She waited for the show.

"Too long to be proper but short enough not to be classified as lethal weapons." Nadine spread her fingers, wiggling each one, admiring their glittering tips. "Aren't they beautiful? Why, every time you look at them, you get a buzz."

Eden smiled. "They're you, Nadine." She gently packed peat moss around a young jade plant.

Nadine walked back to the tea cart and got a potato chip. The crunching sound contrasted with the calm of the shop. Eden felt her friend's study. She looked up and smiled.

"Don't give me that." Nadine bit into the chip.

"Give you what?" Eden wondered if her friend was spending too much time around hair-processing solutions.

"That 'I'm okay, you're okay' smile." Nadine marched to the design table. "What's that they call you—'Even Eden.' Except lately they're saying 'Even Eden Does It.'"

"Nadine!"

The other woman's smile was sly. "At least that got a rise out of you. It beats seeing you hanging around this hothouse all the time, wilting away like yesterday's roses."

Eden wired a pinecone rose to a philodendron. "I'm working, not wilting."

"Honey, you're drying up quicker than a snakeskin in the Texas sun. It makes me just want to sit down and have a good cry after the way you've been skipping around these past weeks, flaunting your title of the Tyler Hospital Harlot."

Eden stiffened. "I don't flaunt."

Nadine licked a salt speck from her finger. "But you were enjoying it."

"Did Tisha wind your rods too tight when she gave you that perm last week?"

Nadine grinned. "It's okay. I'm not going to spread your secret. Besides, I live outside the town limits so anything I say doesn't carry much weight, anyway." She grinned. "Still, that doesn't mean I'm not right."

"My secret?" Eden stopped misting the finished garden.

Nadine placed the tip of a glittering nail on Eden's chest. "Underneath all these still waters, there beats the heart of a sensuous, wild woman just screaming to get out." She folded her arms across her chest, her expression smug.

"A sensuous, wild woman?"

Nadine nodded. "Screaming to get out." She looked around the shop, gestured to the arrangements of velvet red roses and spilling ivy. "Sensuous."

She pointed to the riot of colors clustered together in the corner. "Wild. All this…" She spun around, arms outstretched. "All this—" she faced Eden, her fingernail touching Eden's chest once more "—comes from the heart of a wild, wanton, sensual woman. A woman who found out she was the center of a scandal and smiled."

Eden stared at Nadine, her expression grave. "I didn't smile."

Nadine looked her levelly in the eye. "Inside you smiled. Up until this past week or so, that is. But now something's wrong."

"Nothing's wrong." Eden refused to confess.

Nadine waved her hands. "It's all right. I don't

expect you to tell me. I respect your privacy. It's just that I hate to see you looking like this.''

"Looking like what?''

"Like you went in for a blow-dry and came out bald.''

She had no idea how Nadine knew. She hadn't talked to anyone about it. She'd kept smiling, cheerfully greeting customers until by the time Christy came after school, her cheeks hurt. It was only sometimes, at night, when she was alone, she'd let the sadness in.

"Admit it.'' Nadine leaned toward Eden. "All this talk about you and Dr. Delicious, doesn't some small part of you think it's sort of fun?''

Eden took a breath. "No.'' It was the split second she hesitated that gave Nadine her answer.

"Nails,'' the woman declared once more.

Eden looked at her, confused.

Nadine fanned them in front of her face. "They'll make you feel a little bit naughty and a little bit nice, and they're much less painful and messy than a tattoo. They won't cure what's ailing you, but I bet every time you look down at them, you'll smile. Have the shop's name and number airbrushed on them, and you can write them off as an advertising expense. See, you're smiling already. C'mon, my treat.''

Eden rounded the worktable and kissed her friend's cheek. "Nadine, that's so sweet, but really, everything's fine. I'm fine.'' *Good ol' even Eden.* "And unfortunately, torpedo-length fingernails and flower arranging don't go hand in hand.'' She smiled at her own unintended pun.

Nadine didn't. ''A facial, then.''

''Really, Nadine, everything's fine.'' She picked up the dish garden.

''An eyebrow waxing.''

''Ouch!''

Nadine sighed in frustration. ''How are we ever going to make these rumors about you and the doc the truth, if you won't even try to cooperate?''

Eden laughed. ''The truth? That's as preposterous as the rumors themselves.''

Nadine planted her feet and put her hands on her hips. ''Why? Everybody in Tyler believes Brady Spencer can't get enough of you. Why can't you?''

Eden felt her outward appearance of serenity starting to slip. ''Because it's not the truth.''

''So make it the truth.''

''Why?''

''Because you're in love with the man.''

The dish garden slipped from Eden's hands and shattered. She stared at Nadine, then walked briskly to the back room.

''Eden, I'm sorry,'' Nadine said when she returned with the broom and dustpan.

Eden held up her hand, halting the apology. She moved the broom in steady, neat sweeps. She wasn't mad at Nadine. She wasn't mad at anyone. Except herself for falling in love with Brady Spencer. Like the rest of this town, she'd let herself believe in a fantasy. She'd been a fool.

She swept the dirt and pottery pieces into the dustpan Nadine angled for her. Nadine was right. How long was she going to wait? She'd been waiting her whole life, and what did she have? A successful business she loved, but at the end of the day, she needed more than her propriety and a good profit ratio. She did want a husband, children, family, a home. She did want that "right man" she'd been waiting for. The man she'd mistaken for Brady Spencer.

Nadine emptied the full dustpan in the wastebasket and brought it back to catch the last remains. As she bent toward the floor, she caught Eden's gaze. "You know I'm from outside Dallas where they say everything's bigger. In my case they're referring to my mouth."

Eden shook her head and smiled at her friend. "Maybe a trim."

NADINE SPUN the red vinyl chair around, declaring, "Who's the master?"

Eden stared at her reflection in the wide, round mirror. For the past four hours, she'd been steamed, creamed and colored. Her hair had been twisted up into enough foil spikes to pick up the local cable channel, then conditioned, cut and curled. Nadine leaned forward, pulling down a curl on either side of Eden's face, critically eyeing their length in the mirror to make sure they were even. Satisfied, she released them and they bounced back into the soft curve that now framed Eden's face.

"Oo-la-la."

"You said it, Nouci," Nadine told the brilliantly colored parrot in the cage in the corner. Nadine caught Eden's gaze in the mirror and watched for her reaction.

Eden blinked her eyes made smoky and spectacular with shadows and liner and mascara. She touched the fluffy curls that shimmered with golden highlights. Her fingernails had been expertly filed and painted a frosty pink. Her hair had been cut to her chin, leaving her neck long and exposed. Golden wisps angled and tumbled across her brow, giving her entire expression a come-hither look. She smiled self-consciously at her reflection in the mirror, her lips the red of holiday roses. Could this face in the mirror possibly be the same Eden Frazier she'd been two days ago?

The salon's owner, Tisha Olsen, came over and stood beside Nadine. "I'm glad Judson and I weren't off traipsing around some continent this week." She swiveled the chair, turning Eden left and right. "I would've hated to miss this."

"What do you think?" Nadine asked.

Tisha fluffed her fingers through Eden's hair, tousling the curls even more. "Honey, if I wasn't fully recovered from my heart attack, I'd go into cardiac arrest right here she's so gorgeous. I'm worried about the male citizens of this town, though, when they see her. They'll be dropping like flies in February. And if Dr. Spencer knows the source of their shock is this sweet thing, I'm afraid he's just going to let them suffer.'' The older woman winked at Eden, her features crinkling with good-naturedness.

''Dr. Spencer?'' Nadine dismissed him with a wave of her new nails—turquoise with hot-pink polka dots. ''He's yesterday's news. After today he'll have to take a number and get in line.''

''La dolce vita,'' Nouci pronounced from the corner.

Tisha's arched eyebrows lifted. ''Is that so, Eden?''

Eden met Tisha's incredulous expression in the mirror. ''We're just good friends.''

Tisha shot a glance at Nadine. Eden shifted in the chair, unused to being the source of so much attention.

''Let's get you out of that chair.'' Nadine unsnapped the plastic smock covering Eden and pulled out the white towel wrapped around her neck.

''Eden, do you know how long I've wanted to get my hands on that great hair of yours and those incredible eyes?'' Tisha asked as Nadine swiveled Eden away from the mirror.

''Well, the wait is over.'' Nadine pulled off the smock with a flourish. Eden slid out of the chair, smoothing the cotton jumper she wore. She looked up to see Tisha and Nadine staring at her silently.

''Mon Dieu,'' Nouci commented.

''Nouci, behave yourself,'' Tisha warned the bird.

''What?'' Eden touched her hair, her face.

Nadine took her by the shoulders and turned her back to the mirror. Eden saw what they saw. From the neck up she was sultry and stylish. From the neck down she was shapeless and drab.

"Tisha, I'm free until my 2:00 p.m. cut. All right if I take lunch a little early?" Nadine patted Eden's shoulders.

Tisha nodded.

"C'mon, gorgeous." Nadine smiled in the mirror. "We're going shopping."

"I don't know. I'm still getting used to all this." She patted the ends of her curls.

"Oh, no, you don't." Nadine's polka dot finger-nails rested on Eden's arm. "You're not wimping out on me now, Eden Frazier. I won't rest until you're all trussed up like a Thanksgiving turkey and ten times as appetizing."

As she spoke she ushered Eden toward the door. They stopped at the brass coatrack draped with bright feather boas. "Wait right here. Let me just spritz a little Sin on my passion points and grab my purse and we'll go." She winked at Tisha. "Watch her. She might make a run for it."

The front door opened and Lydia Perry came in. "Tisha, I hope you're in the mood to work some magic today." She nodded hello to Eden standing by the coatrack, then did a double take. "Eden?"

"Zut alors!" Nouci called from his cage.

Eden smiled tentatively, curving her shoulders forward, feeling as foolish as the feather boas flut-tering above her. "Hello, Lydia. How are you?"

"Never mind how I am. It's you who looks fab-ulous."

Eden shyly averted her eyes from Lydia's astonished gaze. "Thank you."

"Absolutely fabulous."

"And that's only the beginning," Nadine announced, reappearing from the back room. "Wait until we get back from our little shopping spree at Gates." She linked her arm through Eden's, a wave of scent surrounding her. "Honey, don't blush. We already took care of that with Perfect Cheek Color in Coral Sensation."

Lydia settled in the chair, smoothed the smock Tisha draped over her. "As I remember, a little spit and polish didn't hurt Molly any, either, when she set her sights on Quinn." Lydia looked up at Tisha. "Okay, sign me up for a complete overhaul, too, if that's the secret to capturing a Spencer man's heart."

Eden glanced at Nadine.

"Eden isn't doing all this to try to impress any man," Nadine corrected. "Especially Brady Spencer."

"Yesterday's news, yesterday's news," Nouci declared.

Lydia spun around in the red vinyl chair to face Eden. "Is that right?"

The phone rang. The other stylist at the sink, shampooing a customer, threw Nadine a helpless look. "Let me just get this," Nadine said to Eden, "and then we'll go."

Lydia was waiting for Eden's reply. "Brady and I are friends," she told her.

The woman's expression turned sympathetic. "It's probably for the best, honey. You'd think after seeing Seth and Quinn so happily married, Brady and Elias would see the light, but I'll tell you... Well, I don't know about Brady specifically, but if he's anything like his father, he's determined to stay single."

Tisha turned Lydia back toward the mirror. She patted the woman's shoulder. "Elias is just scared."

Lydia snorted. "And too stubborn to admit it."

Tisha spread a section of Lydia's hair and checked the roots. "It was hard on the whole family when Violet left like that."

"Can you imagine just up and leaving your three boys?" Lydia shook her head. "Not even teenagers yet, were they?"

"Seth was fourteen, but Brady was only eleven and Quinn seven," Tisha explained. "Seth became the man of the three, of course. Brady, he pretended nothing was wrong, nothing was different. Everything would be fine. And Quinn, well, he was just a baby. It'd break your heart to see them boys trying to act so brave and grown-up."

"I've tried to get Elias to talk about it, thinking it might help," Lydia said, "but he's too stubborn and won't say a word."

Tisha shook her head. "He never would talk about it. Wouldn't let the boys even mention their mother's name. Come on back to the sink, and I'll have one of the girls shampoo and condition you."

Lydia heaved a sigh as she pushed herself up from

the chair. "Hard for a man to move on with all that hurting still locked up tight inside him."

Tisha patted the woman's shoulder again. "Hang in there, Lydia. Elias will come around."

Nadine hung up the phone. She scribbled in the appointment book, then looked at Eden. "Ready?" They headed toward the front door. It opened as they reached it.

"Afternoon, ladies." The express deliveryman, Wayne Donovan, came in, carrying several boxes.

Tisha whistled. "My favorite sign of spring—the express deliveryman in shorts."

Eden looked at the uniformed man. He'd been in her class in high school, although she'd never spoken to him until he began to deliver packages to her shop. She remembered he'd been the homecoming king their senior year, though she hadn't gone to the dance. It was her first thought each time she saw him.

Wayne was only an inch or two taller than her, but strong and square with the contained, powerful carriage of an athlete—not a runner or a high jumper but a shot-putter, a weightlifter. His hair was the rare white-blond born only of genes and sun, and it crowned his head in cherub's curls. But it was the devilment in the man's blue eyes that made him seem to always be smiling and, Eden suspected, accounted for his popularity among both women and men. Now those blue eyes, their merry lights softening, were on her. She glanced down only to confront the man's bared, brown thighs, their force evident even in stance. Yes, definitely a weightlifter, she thought, before looking away.

"It's not that warm out yet, is it, Wayne?" Nadine signed for the packages.

"No, but I love to give Tisha a thrill."

"Careful, I've got a weak heart now."

Nadine rolled her eyes. "She'll outlive us all, won't she?" She looked up from the computerized clipboard, seeing Wayne's interest was elsewhere.

"Wayne, you know Eden, don't you?"

"Sure, I know Eden."

She was forced to look at him, into those dancing blue eyes.

He smiled. "Your hair…"

She touched a curl, pushed it behind her ear.

"I like what you've done with it."

"Honey, you haven't seen nothing yet." With a practiced flip of her fingers, Nadine fluffed the curl out properly.

Wayne's gaze stayed on Eden. "I was on my way to your place next, but if no one's there…"

"The shop's closed on Wednesdays."

"That's right."

"But I can take—"

"You over and unlock the back," Nadine finished.

"Sure." Wayne took the clipboard, his eyes never leaving Eden.

Nadine smiled sweetly at Eden. "I'll wait for you here."

Wayne held the door. With small steps Eden

moved toward it, smiling hesitantly at the ex-homecoming king.

"*Sayonara,*" Nouci sang out.

HE MISSED EDEN, Brady thought. It had been three days. He missed the way her mouth shyly crooked when she smiled. He missed looking into her eyes, trying to decipher their color. He missed her bumblebee slippers and her insolent cat. He missed her.

"You knew we were just giving you a hard time Sunday, didn't you? Us ol' married men, well, we've got to do something for fun." Across from Brady, Seth picked up his coffee cup and took a sip. "That's why I wanted to get together today. I wanted to make sure everything was okay."

Brady knew this lunch date was Jenna's doing. After he had rushed out Sunday night, she had probably insisted Seth set this up to make sure Brady was all right. Seth would've never arranged this on his own. Brady's brothers had learned long ago they didn't need to worry about him. He himself had taught them that. Mothers may leave, fathers may retreat, but his family would never have to worry about him. Brady picked up his coffee cup. He thought of Eden's tea. He shook his head as the waitress approached with the coffeepot.

"Check, please," Seth told her. He smiled at Brady. "So, everything's okay with you, right?"

Brady knew Jenna would require a report. He sipped his coffee, thinking for a mad minute of telling Seth everything—the confusion, the pain, the guilt that'd come again when he learned their mother had died in childbirth only a few months after she'd left them. He thought about telling him how the questions kept circling: What would have happened if she'd lived? Would she have tried to see them? Call them? Sue for custody? Would she have wanted them? Would she have helped them to understand it all instead of burying it as his father had insisted? Would they have understood?

The waitress brought the check. Brady reached for it, but Seth shook his head as he picked up the bill. "I'll take care of this."

Brady watched his brother as he took out his wallet. His brother with a new bride and twin babies on the way. How did it happen, Seth? he wondered. How did you do it? How did you stop being afraid? Afraid of loving someone? Afraid of being left all over again? Brady wanted to know. How do you stop being afraid?

Seth set the check on the table with several bills, took a last swallow of coffee and placed the cup on the saucer. "So, you're okay, right? Everything's fine?"

Brady looked at his brother across the table. "Everything's fine."

"That Flower Phantom business." Seth chuckled. "I guess we deserved that. That was a good one. Except Quinn says Sara still thinks you know Santa Claus personally. He doesn't have the heart to tell her when he was a kid you told him ol' Kris Kringle was a— What did Quinn say you called him? A dangerous propagandist symbol of a materialistic society?'' Seth stood, chuckled again. ''Fortunately, Quinn was only seven and had no idea what you were talking about.''

Santa Claus was only one of a long list of things Brady had stopped believing in when he was young. He pushed back from the table and got up.

Seth clapped him on the shoulder. ''So, everything's okay, right?''

He nodded. ''Everything's fine.''

AS THE ELEVATOR DESCENDED to the basement, Eden tugged on the underwire bra that the blue-haired saleslady said would become her new best friend. ''I don't think I have this on right.''

''Stop fussing.'' Nadine shooed her hand away from the shirt's silky knit. ''You're wrinkling your new shirt.''

Eden squirmed. ''I think that sweet old saleslady was a closet sadist.''

''I know it's a little uncomfortable, but you've got cleavage.''

Eden fidgeted. ''I never knew I wanted it until today.'' She saw her reflection in the elevator's brass doors. She was wearing a white fitted shirt with wide cuffs and a button-down front undone only enough to show a shadow of her recently acquired cleavage. Her black knit pants flared at the bottom but clung to the rest of her. Open-toed slingbacks added three inches to her average height. Silver hoops dangled from her ears. A wide silver band wrapped around her wrist where her cuffs had been artfully rolled back. The look was stylish and sexy. She stared at the woman in the brass reflection. She—Eden Frazier—looked sexy. The elevator stopped. The doors opened. The reflection disappeared.

"Okay, now I want you to strut," Nadine directed.

Eden's laughter came from low in her chest, deep and throaty. Gosh, she even sounded sexy. It had to be the underwire cutting into her esophagus. "I don't strut, Nadine."

"Then, sashay," Nadine instructed over her shoulder as she stepped out of the elevator, balancing shopping bags in either hand.

"Stumbling is the best you'll get from me in these heels." She bent to gather the bags beside her feet but the tiny, ridiculously impractical purse Nadine insisted she buy swung forward, its thin straps tangling around her arm and tightening into a choke hold across her neck.

"Could I help?" a deep voice asked.

She looked up to steady green eyes. They were aimed at her breasts newly born from modern manufacturing.

"Hello, Brady."

Silence. A too-long, deep breath of silence.

"Eden?"

She untangled herself and straightened. She blew out a breath from the effort, felt her sweep of bangs lift, then fall across her forehead once more. "Hi."

The elevator doors began to close. Brady

slammed his hand against one and the doors retreated. He stared. His eyes went from her high-
lighted hair to her cherry-colored mouth to her cor-
seted breasts, then down the outlined length of her
legs to her tiny seashell-pink toenails peeking out
from her sandals. Inch by inch his gaze retraced its
path, till it finally met hers. She knew the woozy
feeling in her head was no longer from the stran-
gling purse.

She adjusted the purse until the strap once again
diagonally separated her breasts. She saw Brady's
throat muscles ripple. He swallowed, but he didn't
speak. She felt a small smile on her own face, but
wasn't sure when it had come. She lifted her bags,
knowing if ever there was a time to sashay, it was
now.

She tilted her chin up, squared her shoulders and
prepared her hips to sway. She stepped out of the
elevator. Her heel caught on the elevator car, and
she fell straight into the solid width of Brady's chest.

He smelled so good and felt so familiar. She knew
the embrace of his arms was an automatic response.
But then they tightened only to immediately loosen,
releasing her, steadying her until there was space
between them.

She could feel the heat on her face clashing with
the color already there. Brady smiled at her. She
smiled back sheepishly. It was as if they both knew
beneath the clothes and the colors and the curls, after
all, she was still just Eden.

Past Brady's shoulder, she saw Seth watching

them. He tipped his head toward her. "Nice to see you again, Eden." She remembered the last time she'd seen him, the curious looks that he'd shot her, the stories that had been circulating. She felt her face heat again.

"In fact," Seth continued, "I've been meaning to stop by and see you at the shop."

"You have?" Eden moved to the safety of Nadine's side. She glanced once, twice at Brady. His gaze remained fixed on her.

"I wanted to send some flowers to Jenna. No special occasion. Just something to brighten her day, let her know I'm thinking of her. Brady here tells me you have the most beautiful bouquets this side of Lake Michigan. Right, Brady?"

Brady nodded, still staring at Eden. His smile was gone. In its place, she saw the frown that had become so familiar in the last few months.

"How's Jenna doing?" Nadine asked.

"Great." Seth beamed. "Healthy as a horse."

"Won't be long now, will it?"

The proud papa-to-be nodded. "She's due in May. We've made it to the home stretch—third trimester."

Nadine smiled wistfully. "You must be getting so excited."

"Excited. Anxious. Overwhelmed at the thought of twins. And of course with the increased risks with multiple births, Jenna and I worry sometimes. Will the delivery go all right? Will the babies be healthy?

Will we be good parents? Those kinds of things. But that's only natural. Right, Doc?''

He nudged his brother. Brady's gaze was still on Eden. ''Uh-huh,'' he answered.

Seth smiled. ''Spoken like a true medical professional.''

The elevator doors opened once more. More customers on their way to the store's basement luncheonette stepped out. From among them came a male voice that said, ''There you ladies are. You didn't have to wait here for me. I would've found you anywhere.''

Wayne Donovan walked over and stood beside Eden. He nodded to Seth and Brady. Seth nodded back. Brady's gaze finally left Eden to glare at the deliveryman.

''Going up?'' An elderly man was holding the elevator door open.

''I've got to get back to the bank.'' Seth glanced at his brother. ''What about you?''

Brady's gaze moved from Wayne to Eden. He nodded, his frown deepening. He stepped into the elevator, his gaze frozen on Eden until the brass doors closed, and he was gone.

Chapter Eight

Eden slid into the booth, her gaze on Nadine. "You set that up."

Nadine propped her chin in her hands, her fingernails framing her face. "Honey, even I'm not that good."

Eden scowled at her, unconvinced.

"Okay, I confess." Nadine pointed one long fingernail over her shoulder toward Wayne who was saying hello to some friends at another table. "I did extend a lunch invitation to Wayne while you were locking the shop back up."

"Nadine!"

The other woman shrugged, unrepentant. "Honey, did you see those thighs? Now we know why his company's motto is We Deliver The Goods." She leaned back and smiled. "Sweetie, you keep blushing like that, and I'll have to use a yellow toner beneath your foundation to counteract the red."

Eden looked at Wayne standing several tables

away. He glanced over and smiled at her. She looked down at the menu. "I'm just not used to all this—the clothes, the hair—"

"The looks?" Nadine's smile turned suggestive. "Darling, did you see Dr. Delicious's expression? Poor man. By the time he left here, he looked as confused as a eunuch in a whorehouse. No, honey, I couldn't have planned that if I tried. It was too perfect."

"Brady was surprised, that's all."

Nadine looked over the top of her menu at Eden. "Brady, dear child, was stunned. Not that it matters. The clothes, the hair, the makeover, they're not for any *man*." A turquoise, pink polka-dotted fingernail aimed at Eden. "It's for you, right?"

Eden looked down at her black-clad thighs, her new bustline. Her old clothes were roomier, more comfortable. Then she saw her reflection flash in the wide silver bracelet, and, for the first time in her life, she liked what she saw. She remembered the expression on Brady's face before the elevator doors met. She had to admit there was something to be said for sexy.

Nadine lifted her water glass. "To you."

Eden picked up her own water, feeling a little silly.

"C'mon," Nadine coaxed. "To you."

Eden touched her glass to Nadine's. "To me."

"I'll drink to that," Wayne said standing beside the table. He looked purposely at Eden. She set down her glass, knew her cheeks were coloring.

"There you are." Nadine gestured. "Slide right in next to Eden here and charm us."

"Eden?" He asked permission.

She looked at his boyish face, his friendly, open smile. He wasn't Brady was her first thought. Her second thought was Brady's dumbfounded expression as he'd left. Her third thought was her promise to herself to stop being such an utter fool.

She smiled up at Wayne as she scooted over. "Please join us."

HE WOULD JUST SAY HELLO, Brady thought as he came out of the hospital and headed up Gunther Street. It'd been almost a week since he'd last seen her. Okay, only two and a half days since their chance meeting outside Gates's luncheonette. Brady still hadn't gotten over the shock. At first he hadn't even recognized Eden wrestling with her shoulder bag in the elevator. He'd only seen that soft golden hair, those clingy black pants, a silky white shirt open at the neck, the smooth shadow of full breasts. Those breasts. He'd not stopped thinking about those breasts for two and a half days.

He would just say hello.

He turned onto Tulip. Spring was in full force now. The ground was still moist, the soil dark and wet but overtaken by newborn growth. Green was everywhere, the branches above, the bushes that only weeks ago were spindly and sad. Crocuses, tulips and daffodils pushed up through the dark earth. The sunlight stayed longer. The world, newly washed, was brighter and more beautiful than ever. It was a season of everything.

The Garden of Eden was dark except for the subtly lit windows and beyond them the lights of the cooler, the fish tank's faint ultraviolet. It was past closing time. Brady glanced up, saw the pale lace of the second-story windows and smiled. He turned into the alley between the shop and the salon, thoughts of sweet smells and soft talk and concealed canvases filling his head as he came to the back door. As if greeting a friend, he wrapped his hand around the doorknob. It didn't give way.

The door was locked.

He tried again, his fingers tightening around the knob's cool circle. It twisted a quarter right, a quarter left. No more. Again he twisted it right, left, right, left as if persistence alone would prove this couldn't be possible. This door had never been locked before when he came.

He stared hatefully at the doorknob. Why would she lock her door?

Of course, she hadn't known he was coming, and he had suggested they not see each other for a while until the sex-in-the-supply-closet scenario faded from Tyler's universal memory. Still, the door had never been locked before.

He knocked once, twice. He pressed his ear to the door. There were no sounds inside. If she was upstairs, she might not hear him knocking. That was why she shouldn't have locked the door. He knocked again. There was no light beneath the door.

He stepped back, looking up at the second-story windows. They were dark, too. She wasn't home? He rubbed his forehead. She'd never not been home before. The door had never been locked before.

Still rubbing his head, he walked slowly down the alley. Locked doors, an empty apartment, Eden out, looking like something you wanted to eat with a spoon? He saw the park new and green. Everything was changing.

He walked to the square and settled on a bench beneath an oak lush with the season. He would wait. Wait until Eden came home and the world righted itself again.

It was almost ten o'clock when the car—one of those pretentious two-seater sports models that seem to run on testosterone instead of gas—stopped in front of Eden's shop. The engine switched off. The minutes went by, and Brady almost convinced himself Eden wasn't in that car. It was two strangers who had randomly parked. Perhaps The Garden's windows drew them as they had once drawn Brady?

Then the driver's door opened, and a man in slacks and a navy blazer got out and rounded the car's phallic-shaped front to open the passenger door. Brady knew it was Eden even before her new curls caught the streetlight. The world had gone mad.

He watched the man sling an arm across Eden's shoulders. What kind of woman went out in a sleeveless dress at this time of year? Didn't she know rhinovirus peaked in the spring? The dress was too thin. Even at a distance, he could see the way it clung to every curve, smoothed across every soft mound.

Was that feminine laughter he heard? The man must have made an inane joke, and Eden had laughed to be polite. Brady knew Eden. She was always polite. The couple turned into the alley. She wasn't going to invite him upstairs to her apartment, was she? Didn't she know that was how crazy stories got started?

Brady got up and headed across the square. What if Eden had asked the man up to her apartment, and Brady had shown up outside her back door late at night? His steps slowed. What would he do? Order flowers? He stopped. What right did he have to interfere in Eden's life?

He stood in the darkness. He had no right. No right at all. She was a young, single woman free to date whomever she pleased. Whenever she pleased.

Over his dead body. He started again toward the shop. When he saw the man in the blazer come out from the alley, he laughed out loud. The man looked around as he opened the car door, then slid inside and drove off in his four-wheeled phallic symbol.

"Sorry, buddy," Brady said as he crossed the street, smiling as the car sped off. "Overcompensating is always so transparent."

He was whistling as he turned into the alley. He saw a light beneath the back door and smiled as he knocked.

"Wayne?" Eden asked.

Wayne. Brady rolled his eyes. "Eden, it's me."

The door swung open. "Brady?"

God, she looked like a dream. She wore deep purple, deeper than her eyes, he thought. Until he looked into them, their depths so dark, he seemed to be falling. The dress seemed to touch her everywhere, moving with the quick inhale-exhale of her breath, rising across her chest, laying flat against her stomach, sloping down her hips to envelop her thighs.

"What are you doing here?" Her lips were painted velvet-red, her eyes were made even more mysterious with midnight-blues and jet-black. Her fingertips were burgundy. She had become her paintings.

"Did you want to send some flowers?"

"Yes. No." She was staring at him, a tiny frown pulling at her brow. "Maybe." He was babbling. For the first time in his life, he didn't feel in control of the situation. And he didn't like it.

She continued to look at him, baffled.

"I'm concerned about you." He took charge again. He was, after all, the doctor.

She looked at him as if he was speaking a foreign language. Of course she didn't understand. He didn't understand himself.

"Concerned about me?"

"Yes...that dress—" His hands combed the air.

"This dress?" She smoothed the material where her waist narrowed, her fingertips ruby against the rich purple.

He swallowed.

"What's wrong with this dress?" she prompted.

"It's too lightweight for this time of year. The temperatures drop at night. Rhinovirus is peaking. You should've at least carried a sweater."

Her stare narrowed. "You've been watching me?"

"I was waiting for you."

"Waiting for me? Where?"

He inclined his head. "In the park."

"You were spying on me?"

"I was waiting for you." He distinguished each syllable.

She looked at him as if she'd never seen him before. "You locked the door," he pointed out.

"I was out."

"I know." He paused to let her explain.

She looked at him with those huge violet eyes. "Of course you know. You were spying on me."

He sighed. "I was concerned."

She folded her arms across her chest. "I like this dress. There's nothing wrong with it."

He looked at her. "I didn't say there's anything wrong with it. I said the next time you go out in it in the early spring, you should take a sweater."

"Thank you. I appreciate your concern." There was a new, teasing note to her words.

"The parainfluenza virus is also running rampant this time of year."

What was she smiling about? Besides the fact he sounded like a jackass.

"I'll remember that. Is there anything else I need to know about spring viruses, or was that your sole reason for spending a Friday night sitting in a dark park?"

"You locked the door."

"I told you—I was out."

"You should be more careful."

"I was being careful. That's why I locked the door."

"No, I mean whom you go out with."

"You mean Wayne?"

He rolled his eyes. "Wayne."

"What's wrong with Wayne?"

"He drives too fast."

"He's got a hot little car, doesn't he?"

He definitely heard taunting in her tone. "He's overcompensating."

She leaned her head back and laughed. He was mesmerized by the slender river of her throat.

"Come on upstairs, Doctor. Have a cup of tea and some cookies with me for all your trouble."

She turned. The dress swirled, then settled, covering her body like a jealous lover. She stopped on the third step and tossed a glance at him over her shoulder. "Are you coming?"

There was a dark gleam in her eyes he'd never seen before, a sureness to her step, a bold way she held herself. He'd never wanted another woman as much as he did her at that moment.

He moved toward the stairs. "I hate tea, you know."

Her laughter floated down to him as she opened the door to her apartment. "Then why do you drink it?"

He came to the doorway. "I don't want to be rude."

She'd slipped off those spine-destroying heels and was flitting around the kitchen like a wood nymph. "You certainly seem to have no problem with that tonight."

"I'm not being rude."

She laughed again. "You've insulted my dress, my date—"

"All I'm saying is you should be more careful."

She stopped dancing around the kitchen and stood before him, so delicate. "Brady, all I did was go out. Go out and have a good time like every other single girl my age does. Goodness, you act like I committed a deadly sin." She shook her head as she turned toward the cupboard, and once again Brady noted how the dress hugged her rounded hips, her behind.

He shifted, swallowed. "I'm concerned."

She whirled round. "You were the one who told me to find Mr. Right."

"I told you to *wait* for Mr. Right."

"I'm tired of waiting. I've waited and waited and waited, and here I am, a twenty-seven-year-old virgin with a hothouse and a cat with an attitude."

He stepped toward her. "Eden, it's not like that."

She waved her hand, dismissing his words with a sweep of sculpted nails. "There's more, Brady, and

I want it. I need it. I've waited too long." The dark purple of her eyes seemed to swallow him. "I'm done waiting."

He searched for words. He had to keep talking. "And the changes in you—the clothes, the hair, the..." His hands, which had performed miracles, hovered helplessly. "The everything. This is all part of it? This is going to get you what you want?"

Her eyes looked deeply into his, and he watched as they paled to violet—still darker in the center, lighter near the edges. He saw everything in those eyes—yearning, desire, hope, defeat.

"You," she said. Her voice was quiet, resolute. Her expression was calm as if a choice had been made. "You were what I wanted. All I wanted. Always. It was you. Never anyone else."

He heard her words, saw her face as if dreaming. He wasn't the right man. They both knew that. Still she wanted him, was brave enough to cock a hip, angle her head, look up at him from beneath blackened lashes and say the words that had been singing in his head, having him stumble around for weeks now.

He pulled her to him so swiftly it seemed she'd never been out of his arms. "I want you, too."

He said it to her with his lips hard against her throat, his body pressed to hers and any thoughts of stopping gone from his mind.

"I want you." His words ground against her flesh as his hands, hungry and desperate, found her, touched her everywhere, and a deep need swirled, drowning him, drowning her. He buried his face against the sweet curve of her neck, hearing his own breath coming too quick. He held on, struggling for control where all was sensation, emotion, chaos.

Calm would not come here, his mouth pressed to the taste of this woman, his hands struggling to be still against the silk of her skin. He ground his teeth together and pushed himself away, pressing his lips thin as the hunger rose, already damning him. Searching for self-control, he managed several inches of distance between himself and the promise that was Eden. Still his hands mutinied and clung to her. He couldn't let her go.

Her eyes were close, looking into his. They were rounds of dark, rich purple now. And in their centers was the certainty he'd been searching for.

She lifted her hand to his cheek, and he was lost. His brave, beautiful Eden. He cupped her hand, pressed it to his beard's rough surface and lowered it to his lips, kissing each fingertip. "Are you sure?" he whispered from the sweetness of her skin.

He felt the quiver in her fingertips. "Please," she asked. Her voice was soft, suppliant, and something inside him broke free, surged through his bloodstream, stilling his own fears, focusing him only on this woman, wanting only to give her pleasure.

He bent low to those uttering lips, his own mouth skimming their surface as his tongue traced their shape, teasing them as they parted, then moving on to her cheek's soft curve, the pulse that beat at her temple. Just as slowly he came back to her mouth, drinking her in leisurely, deepening the kiss slowly, slowly until the betraying tightness of her body and the nervous touch of her hands subsided. Still he stroked the sweet sides of her mouth, his tongue touching hers, exploring it with soft restraint, leading it between his own lips, loving it with gentle pressure. He pulled it full inside him only to release it, follow it, fill her until fear and doubt fell, leaving only a long, swelling desire that twined her fingers around his neck and lengthened her muscles as she seeped into his soul.

He felt the press of her flesh everywhere, the warmth, the wanting; felt the world slow to a gentle song, an elemental rhythm; and knew that there'd been nothing before. Before this night. All else was only prelude. He felt the uptake of desire, physical and potent, but, stronger still was his prayer only to please this beautiful woman before him.

She was pliant as he cradled her in his arms and carried her into the rose-colored bedroom. He laid her down gently onto the bed, then stepped back just to see her in the tender light, her hair like dark honey spilled against the pure white linen. Her eyes had darkened, clouded where desire warred with the fear of a first time. He drew the blinds, dimming the light before he went to her and lay down beside her, his face near to hers as he slowly stroked her shoulders, her arms. She reached for him. He saw the jerk in her muscles. He bent and kissed the inside of her arm, nibbling away its stiff angle.

"Shh." He sought to calm her. "Let me touch

you." His hand, soft as air, smoothed the hill of her hip. "Let me show you how much I want you."

His hands continued to find her while his mouth moved over hers, his lips touching hers as he whispered, "I want you, Eden. I want you."

He tasted the soft shudder of her sigh, felt the flutter of pulse beneath his fingertips as he stroked the vulnerable curve of her neck. He lifted his head, propping himself on one elbow, and looked down on her lovely face. She opened her eyes, meeting his gaze as his hand ventured further, his fingertips teasing the deep curve of her neckline. He felt her body shift, knew the tension in his own muscles. His hand stilled while he steadied his breath, sought the restraint he had vowed to give her. Her breasts lifted, pushed against the silken fabric. His gaze stayed on her, steadying her as much as himself.

Her lips parted in an innocent's smile. "I'm not afraid, Brady." He smiled at her, although they both knew she was lying. There was never sex without fear. He was as scared as she.

He bowed his head, kissed her forehead. He heard her whisper, "I'm a little afraid" and, lifting his brow from hers, looked down at her and fell in love.

He took that mouth once more as his hand slipped beneath the soft material to the swell of her breasts. She turned toward him, filling his hand with her, her body arching with a silent gasp, pushing the hardened point of her to his palm.

His hand left her only to slip the curve of her neckline down, exposing the creamy skin of her shoulders. He unclasped the beige lace that held her breasts, now free and magnificent. His mouth moved from the soft pink of her shoulder to touch a deeper pink bud with the tip of his tongue, bringing forth a new gasp, full-throated and deep. His mouth grazed one, then the other, lazily moving back and forth, knowing there could be no fill, only a prolonged pleasure, a slow, sensual spinning, drawing her, drawing him down deeper as he lost himself in this moment, this woman, wanting her never to want again, wanting only to give her pleasure.

Her hands pulled him tight to her, held him fast. Still he drew her slowly in, feeling the rise and fall of her chest, feeling his fear, her fear dissolve as he drew deeper, harder, giving her the sensation she needed.

He broke free only to stroke her lovely shoulders, gently draw her dress down lower, baring her to her waist. His mouth followed, finding the delicate dip of her stomach, hearing her sharp inhale, feeling the involuntary rise of her hips. He soothed her, slowed her, his palms softly stroking the narrow bones framing her pelvis.

He leaned over her, still stroking, soothing, adoring. "You're beautiful, Eden."

He saw her first flash of disbelief, saw the first self-consciousness draw of her arm across her breasts. Gently he drew her arm away, never letting his gaze leave hers. "You're beautiful." His fingers circled the dusky point slowly, slowly, his eyes steady on hers until the irises clouded, the lids lowered and he saw her enter into the spin of sensations circling her.

He sat up, his own breath too unsteady, his hands trembling as he undid the buttons. He glanced down, saw her eyes were opened, watching him. She pushed herself up, took his hands in her own and brought them to his sides. Her fingers trembled, too, as she finished undoing the buttons, but he didn't stop her, realizing her need to do so. She finished. He pulled the shirt off and wrapped her in his arms, pressing flesh to flesh, feeling her yield, her need.

He laid her down once more as she clung to him, the touch of her hands eliciting a low groan from deep within him.

"Soon," he told her, skimming her skin with his mouth, stroking her flesh. "Soon."

He stood, left her lying alone as he unbuckled his belt, unsnapped his pants. This time she didn't rise to help him, only lay long on the bed, the pulse working in her throat and the vulnerability achingly real in her expression. Naked, he knelt beside her, saw her looking at him. He drew down the soft folds of her dress, the lace and satin of her underwear, still crisp with newness, gently removed the stockings until she was nothing but skin and softness and wide, violet eyes watching him.

He went to her mouth once more, his lips wordlessly working on hers, waiting for her answer, finding it in her tongue's tentative thrust, the sudden plunge of her filling his mouth, then bringing him back to her. His hand glided across the length of her, her fine flesh, finding her hot and damp as he cupped her with his hand, a sudden lift of her hips as she writhed, tearing her mouth away from his to draw deep breaths. Patiently his fingertips circled her once more, his mouth opened against her skin, the strain of his desire threatening.

He felt her own tremble beneath his touch, a tremble of fear and need, a pulse quickening now of ready, waiting desire. He heard her breath, heard his own, drew in deeply while hers quickened, escalated to a moan.

"Please." She was no longer humble; she was demanding. "Please, Brady, please."

He found her moist and tight. She tilted her hips to him and wrapped her arms around his neck as if afraid she would fall.

"Now, Brady. Be with me."

Her thighs had opened. He lowered himself, every ounce of self-restraint seeming impossible but needed now most. She tipped her hips up, and he touched her, easing into the hot, moist folds of her, his body rigid with the desire to thrust hard and greedily. *Don't let me hurt her.* More than anything he didn't want to hurt her.

Her eyes opened, those violet eyes. They stared straight into him with a glazed trust as her hips lifted, welcoming him, wanting him. And he could not breathe. He lowered himself into her so slowly. There was the push of slight resistance, and still her eyes didn't waver but stayed steady on him as her lips curled into a smile. There was the strain of his body as he felt her close tight around him, her eyes clouding, closing, her lips pulling back in pants of desire.

"Now, Brady," she breathed, breaking his brittle restraint, shattering him, and still he eased inch by shuddering inch.

Her head fell to the side. Her hands reached for him, pulling him down, flesh to flesh, parted mouths joining and all barriers broken as he quickened his thrusts. Her legs rose, locked tight around him, drawing him deeper inside her until all dimmed. He felt her fingers in his, holding on, bone against bone, and his muscles, too long rigid, released with a shattering spasm that went on and on and on, carrying him, carrying her home. Their mouths still opened to each other, he heard his own cry swallowed by her great gasps of breath like laughter. Their energy spent, the crisp linens damp, their skin flushed and moist, legs entwined, there was nothing except each other.

Chapter Nine

Eden awoke alone. She stretched, her muscles never having felt so long, the pleasurable ache between her legs new. Sometime in the night she'd slid beneath the sheets and, wrapped in Brady's arms, pretended to sleep until his own breaths had taken on the even rhythm of rest. Then she'd opened her eyes, giving herself the luxury of watching him unobserved, remembering everything, the taste and texture of him, the way he murmured her name, the pleasure. He'd awoken then as if sensing her study and smiled as he placed his mouth on hers once more.

After, she'd slept a child's sleep. Now her arms and legs stretched, reached and found only an empty spot, still warm where Brady had lain. Had he run already? She bolted upright in bed.

He was in the rocking chair, looking large and awkward in contrast to the chair's thin, feminine spindles. The Raggedy Ann and Andy dolls had been laid carefully on the rug. He was fully dressed and sitting still, not rocking. It was he who watched her now.

The sheets had slid away, leaving her bared to the waist. Suddenly self-conscious, she gathered them and covered herself.

"I hope I didn't wake you," he said, his voice low, soft.

She shook her head.

"It's early." A sliver of gray light beneath the blinds showed it was not much past dawn. "You should sleep some more." His voice was still soft, kind.

"You're up. Dressed."

"I'm an early riser." Even in the dawn gloom, she could see him glance away from her as he answered.

So this is what it's like the next morning, she thought. *An uneasy alliance.*

She wrapped the sheet around her as she got up. "I'll make you some tea." As her feet touched the floor, felt for her slippers, she remembered his confession last night when he'd first come, when he'd been angry. She smiled. "I mean coffee. I'll make you coffee."

The shadows had made his expression seem even more pensive, but now a smile came, breaking the clouds gathered there.

"No, stay in bed."

She was standing now, wrapped in the sheet, looking for her robe. She spied it on the back of the rocking chair, cushioning Brady's head.

He stood. "I have to go. Early-morning rounds..."

She looked at him. They both knew it was an excuse to leave. Last night, even before he took her in his arms, she'd vowed she would make it easy for him. He'd given her as much as he could. So much. Today she'd make it easy for him.

She nodded, smiled understanding. "Yes." She didn't say anything else, didn't ask if he'd stop by tonight or maybe tomorrow. Last night was more than she'd ever dreamed. She would dream no more. She sat back down on the edge of the bed.

He came and sat beside her. The bed was without its cover. It had been stripped off during the night, would be soaked and washed today. She smiled up at him. He didn't smile back. His finger found her bare shoulder. He bent and kissed it reverently.

She stopped smiling. For a second she wondered if he would stay.

He lifted his head and met her gaze. His hands caressed her shoulders, skimmed the length of her arms.

She'd vowed she would make it easy for him to go. "Thank you."

"Eden." His hands stilled on her shoulders. He looked deep into her eyes. "There have been other times but...it has never been like that."

She was making it easy for him. He didn't have to lie.

"It has never been like that for me, either. But not because there have been other times, of course."

Her voice was light, amused. *Go now,* she thought. *I'm letting you go.*

He bowed his head, brushed her lips with his. She'd never known kisses could be so lovely, much lovelier than imagined. They could be as gentle as air or hard and demanding, as languid as a hot breeze or fierce and full as if to take you whole. There was so much she hadn't known until last night—how a man could be so hard and strong and also be soft and tender; the pure joy of feeling a man's weight on your own, hearing his breaths quicken, blend into a cry. She parted her lips and breathed him in.

Brady pulled back. She saw desire in his eyes, but she also saw distance. She placed her hand against his cheek, letting him go. He turned his head, kissed her palm.

"It was beautiful, Brady. Beautiful."

His eyes met hers. For a split second there was no subtle reserve, no caution. For a second his eyes were clear. "It was, wasn't it? Beautiful."

She nodded. "Exactly as it should be." She spoke as if experienced instead of a woman newly born.

He took her chin between his finger and thumb, tilting her face to his. He kissed her once more, a long, slow waltz of a kiss, their mouths mating even as their minds questioned. His tongue touched the rim of her lower lip, the edge of her teeth, and her mouth opened, unable to resist the taste and texture of him inside her. Her movements were delicate as if there was so much time even now when she knew their time was over. Reluctantly she released him, turning her head aside to press her cheek against his.

"You have to go," she said, her voice thick and her breaths shallow. "You have to go."

He cupped her face, turned it toward him, his gaze on her for a long moment, her heart still. His mouth lowered, touched hers. He would stay.

THERE WAS THE SUN, full beyond the blinds the next time Brady woke. There was Eden beside him, nestled into the curve of his chest, her tousled hair soft across his forearm. There was a sweetness in the air and beneath it, the lingering scent of sex. The digital clock on the nightstand read 7:58.

Eden stirred only to burrow deeper against him. His body didn't tense. It welcomed her. He pressed his lips to her temple, her curls. His arms wrapped around her, holding her, holding on.

He waited for the urge that would untangle his arms, ease him carefully out of the bed.

The seconds passed, and slowly his arms tightened their embrace, not enough to wake her, only to let her know she was not alone.

Neither was he. Not any longer.

There was a murmur, a shifting of the soft weight beside him. Eden's hands touched him tentatively along the line of his back. She lazily lifted her head. Her hair fell across her forehead. She pushed it back and smiled shyly at him.

He looked into those eyes the colors of night and dawn. The urge to run didn't come. What came was something stronger, undefinable, unreal. It had never happened like this to him. There had been other women, numerous relationships built on want and need, mutual attraction and understanding. No more. He'd constructed his personal life as carefully as his professional career. He'd set his course as a boy and had never faltered.

Now he looked into Eden's eyes, seeing her, seeing himself reflected there. Something was different. It was more than the sweet gift of innocence. It was what had brought him back to the shop with its soft colors and sweet smells. It was what had made him sit for hours on a hard bench in the dark last night. It was what overrode the fear, made him lose control, break every belief, shatter his very self only to bring him back, new and whole.

Eden self-consciously smoothed back her hair again. She nervously looked around, then at him, her smile uncertain. "Morning."

His hand curved to her cheek. She closed her eyes, and her smile became content.

"Marry me, Eden," he whispered.

Her eyes flew open. He had never seen them so round.

She thought she might have imagined it, conjured the voice and the words within her head.

"Marry me."

The man beside her said it again.

"What?"

He laughed, the sound full of life as he took her in his arms, pulled her close to him. "Mar—"

She put her fingertips to his lips. "Oh my God, don't say it again."

She rolled out of his embrace to the other side of the bed and lay flat on her back, staring up at the ceiling. *Okay, you can wake up now,* she told herself.

Propping himself up on an elbow, Brady appeared above her.

She managed a weak smile. "And I thought chivalry was dead." She touched his face. "God, who would've thought you were so sweet?" She glanced at the clock. "I've got to get going. Saturdays can be crazy." She slid out from beneath him and sat up, her bare back to him. She glanced over her shoulder with a perky smile to show him it was okay, she was okay.

"Eden, I'm serious." His green eyes were clear, his expression sincere.

"I know, Brady." She resisted the urge to caress his cheek again. "You're always serious."

"Marry me."

The words echoed within her, and for a heartbeat she wanted desperately to believe he meant them. But she also knew Brady. She knew the teenager who'd been so concerned over a little girl's bruised knees. She knew the detached, competent doctor who smiled as he selected flowers to be sent secretly to those in need. She knew the man who just the other night had tried to kiss away her hurt, whose concern had made him come back once more to make sure she was okay. It was this man she'd asked to stay last night. This man who now, plagued by what he had done, had offered marriage solely out of obligation. It was this man she loved and would let go.

"If anyone should have morning-after guilt around here, it should be me."

He sat up. The bed dipped, rolling her toward him until she felt the still-new texture and hardness of a man's bare thigh against her own. "Is that what you think this is all about? Morning-after guilt?"

She pushed away from him and got up, forcing herself to move nonchalantly. She knew his gaze was on her. The memory of last night, his mouth, his hands, the long, sweet fall, suddenly rushed in, weakening her knees as she reached for her robe. She slipped into it, deliberately resisting the urge to wrap it too tightly around her. She was no longer the virgin.

She faced him. "You were vulnerable, and I took advantage of you."

"I...I was...I was—"

She'd never seen Brady stammer. She sat on the edge of the bed once more and patted his hand. "I seduced you. I'm sorry."

He stopped stammering. For a moment she thought he'd stopped breathing.

"But I have no regrets. And neither should you. Last night was beautiful. In fact, it was perfect. You were perfect. Please, if you feel guilty about taking anything from me last night, don't. You didn't take anything from me. What you did last night was give me an extraordinary gift.''

She started to rise when his hand wrapped around her wrist, pulling her down. He lay her across his lap, holding her tightly in his embrace, his desire immediate and obvious. He untied her robe and it fell back, exposing her.

''It is you who are beautiful,'' he murmured, need already darkening his eyes. His hand slid down between her breasts, across her stomach, up her inner thighs already parted.

''I ask you to marry me, and you turn me down.'' She heard a playfulness in his voice that hadn't been there before, and she knew she had allayed his guilt. Still his eyes were watching her as his fingertips made leisurely trails inside her thighs and she thought she'd go mad.

''I only ask once. Not again.''

She squirmed as the fire flared within her, the desire making her wicked and wanton. Her voice was strangled. ''That's one more time than I ever expected.'' She twisted in his hold and, sliding her leg across his lap, straddled him, pressing her flesh to his.

His hands held her hips, steered her to him. ''Marry me, Eden, and let me make a decent woman of you.''

''The hell with decency,'' she said, crushing her mouth to his.

BRADY KNEW the woman perched on the narrow examining table. A few years ago her son had been brought in for shoulder pain after a hard football tackle. He'd been waiting in X-ray when he'd fallen forward, unconscious. Brady had wheeled the boy directly to the operating room, put him on the table for a quick exam and intravenous line, and within ten minutes opened his belly to remove a ruptured spleen.

"How are you, Mrs. Mattice?" Brady looked up from her chart. He always addressed his patients by their surnames.

The woman smiled. Her face was rounder, softer than he remembered. "Fine, Doctor, except for this pain that keeps pestering me." She placed her hand high on the right side of her abdomen. "I think it's gallstones. My mother had them, and I remember her having similar pain."

He asked more questions about the pain, nodding and making notes on the chart. "Okay, let's have a look." He set down the chart and moved to the narrow table. "How's Joshua doing?" he asked about her son as he helped the woman lie back.

She smiled up at him. "Great, thanks to you. Don't think I don't thank God every night for you and your swift thinking. That's why if I have to have any surgery done, I want you to do it, Dr. Spencer. I trust you."

"Thank you, Mrs. Mattice." The formal address suddenly seemed awkward. He placed his hand beneath her rib cage on the right. "Take a big breath."

She winced.

"That's where it hurts?" He helped her up to a seated position, releasing the bottom section of the table.

"That's where it always starts. Sometimes it moves around to my back, up between my shoulder blades. And it's always worse after I eat fried chicken or chocolate."

He nodded, writing again on her chart. "We'd better run a few tests. We'll let the lab draw some blood and take a look at it. And I'd like you have a CT scan to check for the presence of stones." He heard his voice, a soft, reassuring tenor. "When you're done getting dressed, come on out and my nurse will make the arrangements."

He placed his hand on the woman's shoulder. The "laying on of hands" was as much a part of the art of healing as operations and prescriptions. "If the pain comes and doesn't go away, lasts for over an hour, call me or come in immediately. Promise?"

She nodded.

"And easy on the fried foods and chocolate."

She smiled. Brady headed toward the door.

"Doctor?"

He looked back. The woman's smile was gone. "If I have to have surgery, I want you to perform the operation."

He nodded. "No one gets near that gallbladder but me, Mrs. Mattice."

He handed the chart to his nurse and walked to his office, waiting for the slow spread of satisfaction his work always gave him. He was a good doctor.

He had cultivated all the necessary ingredients: the steely determination, the surgical creativity, the correct balance of emotional detachment and concern, and the always-necessary, almost-arrogant confidence. His patients trusted him; his colleagues respected him. He was a successful surgeon.

He also knew the motivation that had fueled his success. He'd done a psych rotation, but even without his medical background, it was almost embarrassingly obvious: he'd designed his life to compensate for his mother's abandonment. He was a textbook case, but he didn't care. For him, it'd worked.

Until recently.

Until last night.

He sat at his desk, tapping a pencil against its edge. The symptoms had shown up months ago—the secret flower deliveries, the anonymous gifts. Who would ever abandon someone so benevolent? If his mother had been alive, wouldn't she have been proud?

Still the reality remained—his mother had left him, left them all. And she was never coming back. Not now. Not ever. No matter how wonderful a doctor he was or how many people he helped. It didn't matter. His mother was gone. All that remained was the guilt, the anger, the hurt. The empty spot inside him that he'd feared would never be filled.

Until last night.

He pushed away from the desk. He had held women in his arms before and still felt alone, still yearned, but with Eden it wasn't like that. It was as if all he would ever need was the width of her waist, the bareness of her back, her skin turning warm and pink as he rubbed it. It was as if the answer to everything had become the simple length of her body. Nothing more.

That was why he'd asked her to marry him.

He released a long breath. He had to stop, regroup, take hold. Secretly sending flowers was silly enough. Popping out marriage proposals was a sure sign of instability. He'd been crazy to ask. Luckily Eden hadn't been crazy enough to accept. And thanks to her tactful refusal, he'd had time to gather his wits and cover his own embarrassment, disguising how serious he'd been by making light of the situation. Marry Eden? Even now, hours later, the idea was absurd, completely irrational.

And the only thing he could think about.

Mrs. Mattice had been his last appointment, but it was still before noon. The office closed at eleven-thirty on Saturday mornings. He tried to focus on the charts before him, but it was no use. He returned a few phone calls, then gathered his papers. He would work at home this evening. He said goodbye to the receptionist straightening up the empty waiting room as he left.

He walked the long way around the square to Main Street, avoiding The Garden of Eden. He picked up his dry cleaning and was heading home when he saw Seth coming out of the grocery store, a sack in each arm.

Brady shook his head as he came toward his older brother. "Banker's hours, huh?"

"You're one to talk." Seth shoved a bag at him. "Little early in the day for you to be done saving lives, isn't it?"

Brady looked into the bag. "Extraspicy salsa, Marvelous Mocha ice cream." He sniffed. "And four garlic dill deli pickles." He looked at his brother.

Seth shrugged. "Cravings. Bring that bag and come on home with me. I'll give you lunch. Dad will be there, too. He's going to help me work on the babies' room this afternoon."

Brady looked dubiously at the contents of the bag in his arms. "First I want to know what Jenna is making for lunch."

"C'mon." Seth insisted, already walking to his car. "We can use those skilled hands of yours to hang shelves."

"I knew there was a catch," Brady grumbled, setting the groceries in the trunk of Seth's car.

Seth lived on the same street as Elias. His Victorian shared the traditional wraparound porch and gingerbread trim but was smaller than the Spencer family home and boasted light, gay colors and a white picket fence. As Brady carried a bag of groceries into the kitchen, the flowers bursting out of a vase on the long maple table caught his gaze.

He set the bag down beside the vase. He touched the purple velvet of an iris.

"Aren't they gorgeous?" Jenna asked, coming in

from the other room, full and round and smiling. She kissed her husband, stroked his head as he bent and pressed a quick kiss to her stomach.

"Hello, guys," Seth spoke to her stomach.

"Or girls," Jenna corrected.

"Or both," Elias said, standing in the doorway behind Jenna. He spied Brady. "Good, now I don't have to do all the work this afternoon."

"Okay, so I'm never going to live down the fact I was the only Spencer who failed shop at Tyler High," Seth confessed. "Fortunately I do have other talents." He slid his arm around his wife. She rested her head on his shoulder, still gazing at the flowers.

"I know they belong on the stand in the foyer," she said, "but I wanted them here where I could enjoy them, since I seem to spend most of my time in the kitchen. Speaking of which, I better see to lunch." She straightened and went to the table to unpack the groceries. Still she couldn't resist touching a perfect petal first. "Seth had them sent yesterday from The Garden of Eden."

"Are you sure?" Seth, unpacking the other bag, showed the ice cream to Jenna, then waited for her smile of gratitude. "How do you know they didn't come from the Flower Phantom?" He winked at Brady.

Jenna rolled her eyes. "Because there was a card with your name on it."

"Maybe I'm the Flower Phantom. It could run in the family." He smiled good-naturedly at Brady.

"Sure, honey. Oh, good, you remembered the salsa."

"If Brady can be the Flower Phantom, why can't I?"

Jenna ate a spoonful of salsa right from the jar. "You're certainly sweet enough, honey."

"Flower Phantom." Elias snorted. "Probably some publicity stunt for a new business coming to town. Such nonsense."

"Well, if it's another florist, they might as well keep on going. Everybody says nobody does better work than Eden." Jenna ate another spoonful of salsa.

Seth smiled. "She sure does have a lot of admirers around here lately."

Brady still studied the flowers. From the corner of his eye he saw Jenna wag a scolding finger at Seth.

Brady looked at Elias. "Did you ever send Mom flowers?"

Father and son stared at each other. "What the hell kind of question is that?" Elias demanded.

Brady looked away from his father's glare. He shrugged, willing to let it go. Then he looked down, saw the flowers again. Something welled inside him.

He met his father's gaze once more. "I was wondering. Did you ever do things like that?"

Elias stared at him as if he had lost his mind.

Jenna moved to the refrigerator. "I was thinking grilled ham and cheese and some macaroni salad for lunch.'' She took a foil-covered bowl out of the re-frigerator. ''Is that all right?''

Brady ignored Jenna's attempt to end the discussion. ''You know,'' he told his father, ''those romantic things that women like—moonlit walks, flowers, jewelry. I mean I know we're not supposed to talk about Mom but since Coop found out about her death, well, I've been doing some thinking about her.''

''Maybe that was a mistake, then, letting Coop stir things up long finished. Maybe sleeping dogs should just be left to lie.'' There was a threat in Elias's tone.

''But don't you think about it? About her?'' Brady couldn't stop. He wouldn't stop. He had to know. ''Don't you ever wonder what might have happened if you'd gone after her? Why didn't you go after her?''

Elias stared silently at his son.

''Maybe she wouldn't have come back, but we'd have known what had happened to her instead of all those years wondering why we never heard from her. All those years wondering why she hated us that much.'' Brady looked away from his father. He touched a flower. ''We would have known she didn't hate us, she couldn't hate us. She was dead.''

''Brady.'' Seth took a step toward his brother, but Elias laid a restraining hand on his oldest son's shoulder.

''Didn't you wonder, Dad?'' Brady continued. ''Or did you know? Did she want to see us but knew you'd never allow it? Was she alone when she died? And the baby? What happened to the baby?''

The room was silent. There were no answers.

Brady could not be silent. ''Did you ever tell her you loved her, Dad?'' He stared at the flowers. ''Because I don't know if I did. I can't remember.'' His fingertip outlined a petal. ''I can't remember.''

There was silence until Elias spoke, again his voice gruff. ''If your mother didn't know I loved her, that was her problem.'' He turned and left the room.

''What was that all about?'' No longer held back, Seth came toward Brady. ''You know Dad won't talk about it. It was a miracle we got him to let Coop look into it at all. For Pete's sake, Brady.''

Brady dropped his gaze to the flowers, transfixed by their color, shape, ability to exist as if for no other reason than to make someone smile. His fingertip still rested on a petal. ''He should have sent her flowers,'' he said softly.

EDEN EASED THE LAST pompon chrysanthemum into the floral foam and stepped back. She nodded, satisfied. ''Finally. The last order.'' She wiped her palms on her apron. ''What a day.''

Christy, tying a balloon to a basket, glanced over. ''That came out nice.''

''As soon as David gets back, he can take these and we're done.'' Eden checked the clock. ''He should've been back by now, shouldn't he?''

''He probably passed by the Dairy King and

couldn't resist." Christy brushed ribbon scraps into her palm and threw them in the garbage. "They opened for the season today."

Eden picked up the cookie plate from the tea table. "Did you have lunch?" she asked, offering the cookies to Christy.

"Did you?" The teenager laughed. "It was busy, wasn't it?"

Thank goodness, Eden thought as she nibbled on a cookie. Otherwise she wouldn't have been able to avoid thinking about last night or this morning and Brady's proposal.

"Why's David parking on the street?"

Past the display windows, Eden saw the delivery van stopped beside the sidewalk.

"He knows he's supposed to park in the back." Christy walked toward the front. "Wait, that's not our van. It's from Flowers with Flair." She glanced back at Eden. "They probably want to know the secret to your success."

Eden reached for another cookie, watching the driver get out of the van with a long white box and came to the shop's front door.

"Hey, Eden."

She smiled. "How you doing, Ben?"

"Got something for you." He held out the box.

Christy looked curiously at Eden.

Eden set down the cookie and brushed the crumbs off her hands. "For me?"

The deliveryman smiled as he handed her the box. "Only thing that would make me trespass into your territory." He winked. "Gotta go. Got a few more deliveries before the day's done. Business is booming."

Christy rolled her eyes.

"Wait, Ben." Still holding the box, Eden went to the cash register, opened the drawer and took out several bills. "Thanks," she said, pressing the money into the man's hand.

"Thank you." He nodded goodbye.

Eden set the box on the sales counter, toyed with the ribbon.

Christy eyed the box. "I bet it's a bomb."

Eden laughed. "A bomb?"

"Sure." Christy moved closer. "They want to get rid of the competition." She took another few steps. "Aren't you going to open it?"

"First you tell me it's a bomb. Now you want me to open it?"

"C'mon." Christy reached the counter. "Don't you want to see what it is?"

"Not if it's a bomb."

"I was kidding." She tapped the box. "Open it."

Eden untied the ribbon, folded it evenly and placed it on the counter.

"C'mon." Christy was jiggling up and down now.

Eden smiled at the girl, then lifted the box's long white top. She pulled back the green tissue paper. Inside lay red roses nestled in a bed of baby's breath and lacy greens.

"Ooh." Christy sighed. "Who are they from?"

Eden picked up a perfect rose, wishing her hand wouldn't shake so. She riffled the tissue, gently lifted the flowers. "I don't see a card. Oh, wait, here it is."

"What's it say?"

"'Thank you for a wonderful night,'" she read. She turned the card over, looked at the teenager. "It's not signed."

Christy's eyes got big. "Cool!" She looked at the roses. "They're from the Flower Phantom. Isn't that cool, Eden?" She glanced at her boss. "Hey, are you okay?"

Eden looked at the rose in her hand, feeling foolish as the tears streamed down her face. She was unable to stop them.

She shook her head at her own silliness, but when she met Christy's concerned gaze, she was smiling. "No one..." Like her hand, her voice shook. She swallowed a breath, leaned against the counter for support. Still everything remained pleasantly unsteady.

Eden lifted the rose, touched it to her wet cheek. "No one ever sent me flowers before."

Chapter Ten

Brady decided the diagnosis was simple. He was losing his mind. First there'd been his delusion he could save the world—and himself—by secretly sending flowers. He'd called it a whim. He should have gotten help then.

Now it was too late. The deterioration of his mental state had accelerated so that in the past twenty-four hours, fully aware of the consequences, he'd deflowered a virgin, proposed marriage and estranged his entire family. One more spontaneous act and he'd find himself in a rubber room.

He had tried to analyze the situation, hoping for a cure. He knew the breakdown had begun with the news of his mother's untimely death. Children believe in miracles. Brady now realized adults did, too—they just didn't admit it out loud. And somewhere, buried deep within him all these years, had been the hope that he would see his mother one more time.

But his mother was dead.

This was compounded by the recent wave of romance in Tyler, as if Cupid had taken up permanent residence in the Breakfast Inn Bed. The weddings had begun with his own brothers, for goodness sake, and showed no signs of slowing down. Every Sunday for the past four months, he'd been surrounded by newlyweds, their blissful state a walking billboard for matrimony. Any red-blooded bachelor would snap under such conditions.

And then, there was Eden. Sweet, shy, wonderful Eden with her cookies and her cat and her clumsy slippers. She was so different from the type of woman he'd dated in the past. She was innocence and gentleness; yet, beneath it all, pure passion. Even now, distanced from her and her quiet charm, he couldn't deny something inside him wanted to make her happy.

It was she who had understood that his proposal was only a knee-jerk reaction to morning-after guilt, an impromptu attempt to make amends. She knew him well. Even better than he knew himself, it seemed. Thank goodness one of them had remained lucid.

Because at the time when he'd proposed marriage to Eden, he had been serious. Fiercely, irrationally, ready-to-get-down-on-his-knees serious.

More proof of his deranged state.

Finally there'd been the confrontation with his father today in Seth's kitchen, the emotions roiling and spilling over until he'd destroyed the precarious balance of well-being within the family. A balance that he'd worked so hard all these years to keep intact.

There...he'd analyzed each of his erratic actions. Recognizing and accepting the problem was the first step to recovery. He sat back, planning a course of action.

Tomorrow at Sunday dinner, he would apologize to Elias. Monday he would talk to Eden, who would agree their friendship was too important to risk with further physical involvement. Once everyone realized they were just good friends, the stories about them would stop as quickly as they started.

The Flower Phantom would retire, of course. The unsolved mystery would become nothing more than another interesting story for Tyler residents to tell future generations. Brady would rededicate himself to medicine, approaching it with a fresh energy and the emotional detachment necessary for his professional and personal survival.

Yes sir, in no time, Dr. Brady Spencer would be back to his old self, and life would be back to normal. It had been touch-and-go for a while, but now he was going to stop all this crazy behavior.

He got up to get a beer to celebrate the imminent return of his sanity. The phone rang as he popped the can's top and poured it into an iced mug.

"Dr. Spencer," he said, lifting the mug to his lips.

"Brady?"

"Eden." The sweet, hesitant sound of her voice only added to his feeling that all was right with the world. No matter how close he'd come to professional and personal disaster, he would never regret that his walk on the wild side had brought Eden into his life.

"Brady." There was a pause. Then he heard her say "Yes."

He took another sip of beer, enjoying its cool, tart taste as it trickled down his throat. "Yes?"

"Yes." There was only the sound of Eden's breath.

"Yes?" he said once more as if it were a game.

"I'll marry you."

The mug slid from his hand, smashed against the tile floor.

"Brady? Brady?"

"You'll marry me?" His voice cracked on the second syllable of *marry*.

"Surprised?"

He heard happiness in her voice. "Surprised, yes." He didn't lie. "But this morning…"

He heard a soft laugh. "How could I resist the Flower Phantom?"

He'd been trained to stay cool and calm in emergency situations. He relied on that training now. He swallowed, gained his voice. "I don't know." His voice showed no sign of the shock threatening to tackle him and his newly achieved goal of sanity.

"I've never told anyone this before…" Eden's voice was actually coy.

Oh, boy, he thought. Not revelations. Revelations were never good. "You don't have to tell me, Eden."

"I know. It's crazy. I mean who would have guessed no one ever sent me flowers?"

He tried to understand, tried to make logic of this most illogical conversation. "Well, actually it makes sense since you own a flower shop. It stands to reason that everyone would assume flowers are the last thing you'd want to see at the end of the day."

"Exactly. That's just the point."

"It is?" God, her voice was happy.

"You see, for as long as I can remember, I've loved flowers. When I got older, I dreamed one day someone would send me flowers. But, well, no one ever did. So, I know it sounds silly but that's why I opened my own flower shop. Now I have all the flowers I'd ever want all the time. Plus I help create a happiness I'd never had. You are the only one who ever understood that."

He was? Brady furrowed his brow. "Because I was the Flower Phantom?"

"Exactly. You understood how a simple thing like flowers could make a person's whole world better. You're a good man, Brady, and beneath that strong exterior, nothing but a big cream puff. And, Brady?"

He was hesitant to ask. "Yes?"

"Today you made me the happiest woman in the world. You made all my dreams come true."

He cleared his throat. "I'm glad, Eden." She was right—he was one giant cream puff. A cream puff who couldn't bear to hurt the woman on the other end of the line.

"Would you like to come over?"

He heard the suggestion in her voice, remembered the warmth and sweetness of her, the moment of falling apart in her arms, then coming back complete and new.

"It's late."

"It's eight-fifteen."

"But I didn't get much sleep last night."

"Oh, yeah." He heard the sweet release of her laugh. "That's right. Maybe tomorrow?"

"Tomorrow I have dinner at my father's."

"Oh."

He heard the silent question. Of course, it would seem odd not to invite your new fiancée to Sunday family dinner. He feared he had hurt her feelings.

"Would you like to come?"

He was rewarded with new excitement in her voice. "I'd love to. What should I wear? I'll bake some cookies, unless you think your family would prefer a cake. I know. I'll wear my new wrap skirt. No, maybe just a simple sweater and pants would be more appropriate."

The phone propped against his ear, he listened to her chatter and was glad he'd invited her just to hear the happiness in her voice once more. It would also give him the chance to straighten this all out tomorrow when he could talk to her in person. He didn't want to tell her over the phone that he had changed his mind. No, that was definitely not the way any self-respecting Flower Phantom would handle this situation.

HE ARRIVED EARLY but she was already waiting for him, sitting on one of the two white wrought iron benches that graced the front of The Garden of Eden. She stood, smiling. The sweater set she wore was the color of her eyes; her thin linen pants fitted her slim silhouette. She lifted a hand in greeting, then stayed standing, elegant and poised. It was only her hands wrapped together, clenching and un-clenching, that gave her nervousness away. The day's sun slanted across her, fell on the flowers in the windows framing her. She was all softness and light, standing in front of her garden. He knew she could break as easily as the blooms behind her.

He felt the dull ache inside, near his heart, as he thought of the mistake he'd made and now must undo. He searched for the detachment that had saved him so many times before. He came to her. She stood on tiptoe and kissed his cheek. There was no detachment, only feeling, always feeling with Eden. It was what he feared most of all.

He stepped back, putting distance between them. "I'm early."

"And look at me." Her hands brushed her sweater, the front of her pants. "All ready, sitting here waiting." Her laugh was light, but he heard the uneasiness beneath it. She was as nervous as he. Only he'd been schooled not to show it.

He touched her elbow and just as quickly took his hand back. "We should talk."

She glanced at him but sank gratefully to the

bench. "Yes, there's a lot to talk about. Everything's happening so quickly."

She moved the tin and the bouquet of tulips on top of it so he could sit next to her. "I made cookies. And I thought these might be nice for the table." She fiddled with the edge of the tissue paper wrapped around the bouquet of spring flowers. She looked at him. "I'm so nervous."

His hands, trained to give comfort, automatically touched hers. "Don't be."

She sat erect, as if a deep breath or a sudden movement would shatter her. Her hands clasped and unclasped in her lap.

"But, yes, everything is happening rather quickly," he agreed. He took a breath.

"I know." She turned her head and looked at him with those beautiful eyes. "It's like a dream. I keep waiting for someone to wake me up. Things like this, they just don't happen to someone like me."

In the depths of her eyes he saw the faith and trust.

Her one hand found his. "I'm sorry that I doubted you in the beginning. It's just that everything was happening so fast, and you'd been so concerned, so worried about my feelings, that I thought your proposal was only a gentlemanly gesture. Then later, of course, I realized an honorable man wouldn't make such an offer unless he was sincere."

She touched his cheek. "You've made me the happiest woman in the world, Brady." She leaned forward and kissed his mouth. "I love you."

She whispered those words, and something filled him inside. Something warm and wonderful. A long-forgotten yearning. A need as overwhelming and frightening as it was fantastic. It was what he'd experienced in her bed, in her arms. A sense that this woman, her touch, her smile, was everything. There was nothing else. No need. No pain.

He looked into her magical eyes. She blinked, and all his misgivings and doubts disappeared. Exactly like when they lay together. Before, there had only been fear. The fear that if he cared too much, it would all be taken from him. In a moment. Come home one day, open the door, and without warning your life is never to be the same. He'd known it once. He saw it happen every day at the hospital.

But in Eden's arms, he'd learned there were miracles, too.

He looked at her. This woman who said she loved him, and he knew he would do anything to make her happy. Anything to keep her from being hurt. He looked at her lovely upturned face, and for the first time in his life, he wasn't afraid. He bowed his head and kissed this miracle, tasting sweet fate.

"Let's go," he said, standing. He curved his arm around her shoulders. "Let's go tell the family."

Brady saw Elias alone, rocking on the long porch, reading the Sunday edition as they drove up to the gray Victorian. For so many years his father had been alone. But once, as a young husband, he must have felt as flush and hopeful as Brady did now. Certainly he had never expected his bride would run off, leaving behind him and their three boys. Certainly he had never expected to end up like this—alone in a house too big and too grim. Brady remembered yesterday's accusing words and was ashamed.

"I should have made a cake. No, a pie." Eden fretted beside him.

He parked and smiled at her, determined to ignore the doubts that had started at the sight of his childhood home. *Doubts are only natural,* he reminded himself. *Marriage is a big step.*

They got out of the car. He took the cookie tin, while Eden carried the flowers. With her free hand she reached for his. He laced his fingers through hers and smiled at her. "It's going to be okay," he told her. *It's going to be okay,* he told himself.

He waited until his family was all gathered around the dinner table. Eden was next to him. His brothers and their new wives surrounded them on either side. Molly wiped gravy off Sara's cheek. Jenna leaned back, resting her hands on the curve of her stomach. Elias sat at the head of the table. Before the others had arrived, while Eden was busy putting the flowers in water, Brady had apologized to his father for his behavior yesterday. Elias had accepted his apology with a curt nod, waving his hand when Brady had attempted further explanation. End of discussion. Still an awkwardness remained. Elias had stayed quiet all day. Brady's brothers, too, were unnaturally reserved. There'd been the curious looks directed at Eden when they thought she or Brady were unaware, and, for the first time in several months, too much silence at the Sunday dinner table.

Brady reached for Eden's hand beneath the table and wrapped his fingers around its slender warmth. Sitting here, seeing his brothers' happiness, he felt the doubts that had surfaced earlier begin to fade. He looked at Eden. She was nothing like his mother. In fact, she was the exact opposite. She would never leave him.

"Still planting?" Jenna asked Elias in another attempt to keep conversation going.

Elias looked at her, his gaze vague, his thoughts obviously elsewhere.

"Dad's been getting the garden ready," Brady explained to Eden.

She smiled. "The early thaw has given gardeners a head start this spring. What have you planted, Mr. Spencer?"

"Elias," he corrected. He scratched his head, his manner still preoccupied. "Some green stuff."

There was subdued laughter. "This is a new venture for Dad," Brady told Eden. "He usually just has the boy who does the lawn mow it down when it gets too unsightly."

Elias shook his head. "Not always. My wife, Violet..." His voice trailed off. The tension present all day increased. It was the first time in over twenty years Brady had heard his father say that name. A name that still caused silence.

He held on tight to Eden's hand. Now. He had to say it now, before the silence around him, inside him, gave way to doubt and fear. He didn't let go of Eden's hand. "Ready?" he whispered.

"No."

He gave her hand a squeeze, giving back some of the strength she gave him. "Eden and I have an announcement to make." The silence had continued too long, and his voice sounded unnatural.

His family looked at him, at Eden, their curiosity instant.

"We're getting married."

There was a beat of stunned silence, then everybody was talking. Molly was first on her feet, rounding the table to hug Eden. Although simple acts such as getting up from the table had taken on a new difficulty for Jenna these days, she was right behind her sister-in-law, arms outstretched.

The rest of the family gathered around the couple, and for several minutes there were only hugs and kisses and excited chatter. Only Elias remained seated. He tapped his butter knife against his water glass, signaling for quiet.

Everyone turned to him. He looked at his son. "So, this is why you've been acting so strange lately? After these two—" he nodded at Seth and Quinn "—you'd think I'd recognize the symptoms."

Seth and Quinn looked at each other. "Hey—"

Elias waved away their protest. "The rumormongers weren't wrong this time."

Eden turned to Brady.

"Let's just say they were premature," Brady explained. "In the beginning Eden and I were just good friends."

Seth and Quinn looked at each other and rolled their eyes. Jenna nudged Seth with her elbow. Molly gave Quinn a warning look, but both women were smiling.

Elias regarded the couple. "Friendship is good. It's a firm foundation. You need a good foundation if your marriage is going to last." His sober gaze looked beyond them now, and Brady knew he was no longer talking about the future but the past. He saw a sadness, a regret in his father's eyes that he'd never seen before. For a second it scared the hell out of him.

Elias pushed back from the table and stood, lifting his wineglass. "To Brady and Eden. Much happiness."

The others reached for their glasses and toasted the couple.

Eden looked at Brady. He saw the happiness in her eyes and once more felt strong and unafraid, certain nothing could ever tear them apart. It was only this house, the memories, his father's own obvious regret that had made Brady doubt. He gave Eden a kiss on the forehead. She would never leave him.

Mrs. Eden Spencer. Ms. Eden Frazier-Spencer. Dr. and Mrs. Brady Spencer.

Eden picked up a daffodil. "Hello, I'm Mrs. Spencer." She spoke to the flower's sunny face.

"Yes, I am married to Dr. Spencer, brilliant surgeon and former Flower Phantom."

She traded the daffodil for delphinium, gazing at its budded length. "A baby you say? Are you sure? Oh, my husband, the doctor, will be so happy."

She stuck the flower back with the others and spun around once, letting her laughter echo through the empty store. She couldn't remember a time when she'd been happier.

Brady seemed happy, too. At times he became preoccupied, even distant, but that was Brady. Within minutes he'd snap out of it and seem content once again.

The front door opened, and Eden's smile broadened as she saw Gina. She'd called her friend first thing Monday morning and told her the news. Even then, with Gina's nose for news and the way word spread in Tyler, Eden wouldn't have been surprised if her friend already knew about the engagement. But for once Eden had scooped the star reporter.

Gina's smile was equally big as she came into the store. She spread her arms as she headed toward Eden. "Come here. Give me a big hug."

The friends embraced. Gina stepped back, still holding Eden's hands in hers. Her eyes were moist. "I told you what goes around comes around," she said, referring to the reunion Eden had masterminded Valentine's Day weekend between Gina and her first love, K.J. The weekend had ended in the couple's engagement. Gina winked at Eden. "Thank goodness for universal karma, huh?"

She hugged Eden again. "I'm so darn happy for you. Everybody is. The whole town is talking about you and Brady, but that's not exactly news now, is it?"

"At least this time the talk is true." Eden led her friend to the table and chairs in the corner. "Still you'd think they'd be tired of us by now. Hopefully they'll find something else soon to interest them."

"How about if the identity of the Flower Phantom is revealed?" Gina wriggled her eyebrows. "Do you think that would draw some of the spotlight?"

Eden laughed as she poured tea. "Haven't you given up on that story yet?"

"Are you kidding? Mysterious do-gooder. It's got human interest written all over it."

"You can torture me all you want, but I told you I'm not telling you who the Flower Phantom is. That's privileged information." She smiled as she slid the sugar bowl and creamer toward Gina.

Gina spooned sugar into her cup. "You can't blame me for trying, but I know you'd never betray a customer's trust." She looked up as she stirred her tea, a hint of smugness in her smile. "I understand completely, especially considering there's a personal involvement."

Eden eyed her friend. "What are you talking about?"

Gina grinned. "Eden, you go, girl." She raised her teacup. "To the femme fatale of Tyler, adored by doctors and flower phantoms alike." She took a sip of tea. "But don't worry. As much as I'd love to, I'm not going to uncover our infamous Flower Phantom. Even Tyler needs a mystery. And, unfashionable as it may be, I have my ethics, too. Just like you.''

''You don't know who the Flower Phantom is,'' Eden challenged. ''You're just still trying to get it out of me.''

Gina pretended to be insulted. ''What? You think you're my only source?'' She unwrapped a muffin and sliced it down the middle.

Eden looked at her friend, trying to determine if she was telling the truth or teasing her. ''If I didn't tell you, who did?''

''You know a good journalist never reveals her sources.'' Gina spread butter on a muffin half. ''Let's just say, not all delivery people are as loyal to the florists' unwritten code of ethics as you are.''

''I'm the only one who delivered those orders, Gina.''

The other girl raised an eyebrow. ''Not all of them.''

''All of them.''

Gina shook her head.

Eden stared at her, thinking. Realization dawned. ''Except the last one. Is that how you found out? From Ben at Flowers with Flair?''

Gina winked. ''You'd be amazed what people will do for a slice of Marge's apple pie. Now, don't look so upset. This secret will go with me to my grave. I have to admit, though, it was the last person I'd have thought of. I was positive it was a woman.

And I don't know but he just didn't fit the Flower Phantom profile.''

"There's a Flower Phantom profile?" Eden asked.

"But I guess you don't really know someone until you talk to him," Gina concluded.

Eden thought of all the warm, wonderful conversations she'd shared with Brady.

"So I talked to him."

"You did?"

"Yeah, he's a great guy." Gina took a bite of muffin and chewed.

"You didn't think he was before?"

"I didn't really know him before, except to see him racing around, looking harried and all official. Especially at Christmastime."

"Christmastime?" Eden frowned, confused. "I guess that's a tough season for what they do."

"Yeah, but it's not like the world is going to stop revolving on its axis if they calm down a bit. I mean, those guys give you the impression they're the right hand of God."

"What they do is crucial."

Gina studied her. "No wonder he liked you so much."

"Liked me? I'm hoping he still does."

Gina chewed on her muffin. "Sure he does. But once he heard you were engaged to the doc, he knew he'd missed his chance. Of course, he didn't know about the engagement before he sent the roses."

Eden set down her teacup and gaped at her friend.

"He had it all planned out, you know." Gina spread butter on her other muffin half. "Told me all about it. First he wanted to surprise you with the roses because he knew women loved that sort of thing. Naturally, he would know that, him being the Flower Phantom and all."

Gina balanced the butter knife across her plate. "Then he was going to call you Monday or Tuesday and ask you out for next Saturday night. He didn't want to scare you off by being too anxious or anything like that. But by Monday the news of your engagement was out, and he knew the best thing to do was leave you lovebirds alone."

Eden stared at the other woman. "Gina, who are you talking about?"

Gina took a bite of muffin. "The big F. P."

"And that would be who?" A dreadful thought was forming in Eden's mind.

"C'mon, you know who sent you the roses last Saturday."

"I thought I did."

Gina laughed. "Of course you do. You're the only other person who knows who the Flower Phantom is."

"Tell me who sent those roses, Gina." Both women heard the uncharacteristic urgency in her voice.

"You know as well as I do it was Wayne."

"Wayne?"

"The express delivery guy."

"Wayne Donovan sent me the roses?"

"Yes. Who else?"

Eden got up, paced in a tight circle. "Are you sure?"

Gina's expression turned concerned. "I talked to him the other day when he dropped off some packages in the newsroom. All off the record, of course. Don't worry. I'm not going to reveal his identity."

"I know that." Still Eden's voice was defeated.

"Then what's wrong?" Gina got up and went to her side. "Did I do something?"

"No, no," Eden reassured her. "It's me. I've made a terrible mistake."

Chapter Eleven

Past the twisted oaks sheltering Gunther Street, clouds veined the settling sky. The sun had been crisp and bright, but now rested. Brady noticed everything—the air, the light, the greens and golds all around him, his thoughts like the breeze. There was so much he hadn't seen until recently. So much he hadn't felt...until Eden.

An energy in his blood, he sprinted the last two blocks toward home. He would shower, change and go to her. At the corner, he could already see the tall, modern buildings of the condo complex at odds with their small-town surroundings. Reaching the courtyard's walkway, he slowed to a trot. It was then he saw Eden sitting on one of the backless benches angled at the building's entrance. His easy pace quickened, his smile became full as he unashamedly ran toward the woman he would marry.

Yes, he was going to marry Eden. The decision had been made. The die cast. Not to say there hadn't been moments of misgivings. Times when he had consciously pulled back, and his affections had become cautious. Too many years he'd lived with the pain, the fear of loving and being left. For too long he'd vowed never to feel that pain again. And even though he fought it, the fear had filled him again the past few days, forcing him to restrict his contact with Eden to only brief calls. He knew he was scared. He knew the source, knew the consequences. Still he couldn't stop his withdrawal.

Then something happened those days without Eden. A loneliness came, so vast, he could no longer be alone. Never before had he minded solitude. He'd preferred it, having learned early to take care of himself. All these years he'd taught himself not to need anyone else. And he never had until now.

So he'd surrounded himself with people, patients, colleagues. He'd stayed late at the hospital, taking extra shifts, avoiding his solitary apartment, his isolating office, yet it didn't matter. He was still alone.

Without Eden.

It was then he realized part of him—the very best part of him—no longer resided within his bones and blood. It belonged to Eden. He belonged to Eden. There he would stay.

He reached her, panting lightly, and throwing his briefcase on the bench, pulled her into his arms, spinning her, kissing her, the spring air wrapping about them, the taste of promise on her ripe lips.

"Brady." Her voice was as breathless as his own exhales. "Brady."

No, he didn't want to talk. He wanted only to

stand here in the courtyard and feel the spring and the softness of Eden's lips beneath his. And so he kissed her silent.

Every life has moments never forgotten. Brady had learned that long ago. Moments that remained lucid and new long after they'd passed; moments when everything that happened until then was Before, and everything that came next was After. Such was a moment on this fine April day with the sun and the spring and his heart so full. He knew he had never been happier.

He slowly, reluctantly released Eden's lips, but his eyes stayed closed and his brow rested on hers as he reveled in the taste and touch of her. What more could a man ask for than one perfect moment, and once it was his, how could he not yearn for it over and over?

"Brady."

There was a pained plea in her voice. So discordant was the sound, it stunned him. He went still, already wary. Quickly he dismissed his unwelcome reactions, certain their source was only his long-ingrained fear not yet completely conquered.

"Brady."

He heard it again, the harshness of sorrow, and still he prayed it was his unconscious playing tricks on him. Eden's palms pressed against his chest, pushing him away from her.

He looked into those eyes where he had lost himself. Their color, always unreal, had again changed, turned a shade he'd never seen before. An ominous shade. He no longer felt foolish or firm in his euphoria. He felt nothing except, once again, fear.

Eden looked away, but not before he saw her own expression crumble as if she were a patient who'd just been given bad news. Only this time Brady had the feeling he was the patient and the news was for him. Damn all feelings.

"Let's go up to my apartment." Whatever it was, he wouldn't hear it here, not with the spring warm on his skin. He picked up his briefcase. She didn't protest when he took her elbow. His steps were measured, his shoulders level. He'd been doing it his whole life. It wasn't so hard to again pretend he was invulnerable. They went into the building and rode the elevator in silence, staring at the floor numbers as the lights changed.

Eden saw Brady's hand was steady as he inserted the key. Still she knew he'd sensed something was wrong. When he'd swooped down on her outside and taken her in his arms, she'd almost wavered, had almost believed he loved her.

Then she'd remembered his honor, his ethics that had earned him the respect of his patients and the community; his code that wouldn't permit him to betray another as he had once been betrayed.

He opened the door to his apartment and stepped aside so she could enter. It was her first time here. Brady had always seemed to prefer her cramped place, completely opposite from the room now surrounding her. His furnishings were expensive and so unobtrusively appointed, they must have been selected by a professional hand. The leather couch and matching chair were the green of money; the walls were cream. The wood floor was whisky-colored, the rug on it thick and patterned in dark geometric forms. The entire place had a strength and a masculine sense, but in its careful presentation, without spots or clutter or even a lampshade slightly cocked, there was no evidence of life.

"Sit down," Brady offered. "I'll get us drinks."

He was formal now, further confirming Eden's certainty he'd sensed something was wrong. He was back to the Brady of old—remote, disconnected, polite. She was the cause, and as such, would be the last to blame him.

Then she heard him mutter as he moved toward the kitchen with the glossy tiles, "It won't be any damned tea, either." And she hoped maybe, after it was all over, he wouldn't try so hard to hide the kindness, the vulnerability he shared with the rest of humanity. Maybe, just maybe, he would stay in the human race.

She was still standing, feeling ridiculously awkward, when he came back in with an opened bottle of dark-red wine and two glasses.

He gestured with the glasses toward the couch. "Sit down."

She followed him to the couch as he set the wine and glasses on coasters atop the metal-and-glass coffee table. She tried to perch on the sofa's edge, but the cushions sank with a dignified sigh until she was in their cool, smooth embrace.

Brady poured the wine, handing her a glass without asking her preference. He shifted his body toward her, his posture stiff. "Shall we drink to us?"

She looked at him, remembered falling asleep in his arms, his heartbeat the last thing she knew. She remembered everything as he sat before her, taut and composed. Dr. Brady Spencer, the man everyone admired and trusted, and rightly so. But, as Eden sat there, thinking back, she realized it was the glimpses of his imperfections, his flaws, his very humanness that had made her love him the most. Before she had been in love with the image; now she loved the man.

And because she loved him, she had to know. She had to know if the marriage proposal had been a mistake, an offer rashly expressed, as she'd first suspected, resulting from Brady's elevated sense of responsibility and almost archaic sense of honor. An offer she had quickly recognized for what it was, only to resurrect it once more when she'd mistakenly thought Brady had sent the roses.

"You're not drinking." Brady watched her.

She set her glass on the coaster. Her mind was cluttered already with conflicting emotions. She didn't need the additional fuzziness of alcohol.

"I owe you an apology."

He sipped his wine, his abilities to stay focused and unemotional not in question. "You do?"

"I'm afraid I mistakenly put you in a compromising situation."

His laughter was unexpected and scattered her composure further.

"But they whisper it was I who took advantage of your innocence."

"Except the truth is you've been nothing but a gentleman. A gentleman." She averted her eyes, not realizing the pain would strike so soon.

"Tell me what's wrong."

Had she imagined it or had his voice gotten gentler? She looked at him. "Saturday, right before the shop closed, I received some flowers."

She saw him ready to ask what was unusual about that and lifted her hand, halting his questions. He was too near, and if she didn't continue quickly, she would falter and marry him, no matter what the consequences.

"These flowers were different. They came from Flowers with Flair. Red roses in a white box. A dozen wrapped in tissue, the box tied with ribbon. I've done hundreds of such orders, long-stemmed beauties in white boxes sent out to hundreds of women—young, old, single, married, blond, gray, brunette." She was speaking too fast, her words stream-of-consciousness. If she paused to think, she would never continue.

"All different kinds of women now sharing one common bond. Each had received roses, roses symbolizing, celebrating someone's feelings for them."

"Eden—"

She held up her hand again. "As I said, on Saturday, a dozen roses were delivered from Flowers with Flair, but they weren't for someone else. For the first time those roses were for me."

Emotion stopped her.

"The card said 'Thank you for a wonderful night.'" He didn't understand. "The card wasn't signed." Slowly comprehension came into his expression.

"I thought the roses were from you."

He shook his head slowly.

"And I got carried away and called you, telling you, yes, I would marry you." She closed her eyes, releasing a dry laugh so unlike her. "My goodness, it's a miracle you didn't end up in the Cardiac Care Unit."

She felt him shift and opened her eyes. He had set down his wine. He looked at her. "I'd asked you to marry me that morning."

"Something we both knew was an overreaction to your unfailing duty to do the right thing."

He said nothing, neither denying nor confirming. So she continued.

"Then I called you up, gushing like a teenager..." He shook his head, but she wasn't persuaded. "And what could you do? I know the oath, Brady. 'First do no harm.' I'm sorry."

"Don't apologize."

"I realize now it wasn't the first time I'd put you in a such an awkward situation." She remembered how she'd wanted him, how she'd made it so obvious, so pathetically obvious. She knew he remembered, too. "The consequences certainly weren't the magnitude of a mistaken marriage, but the circumstances were the same.'' She spoke of those nights in remote language even as her face heated. ''I realize you didn't want to hurt me, not then, not now. I know we care about each other, but certainly not enough to base a marriage on. I'm just thankful I found out about my mistake before we made a bigger one.''

Brady sat, his hands resting on his long thighs, his gaze looking straight ahead. Finally he looked at her. ''Who were the flowers from?''

''Wayne. The express deliveryman.''

He nodded, his head turning, his gaze again shifting away from her. He reached for his wine, took a sip, placed it precisely on the coaster. He folded his hands and loosely laced his fingers like a rational, reasonable man.

In reality he didn't know what he felt, so unaccustomed was he to these feelings that raced through him, rising and then just as quickly being replaced by totally opposite emotions. A man who didn't love Eden, who didn't want to marry her would feel relief, but it wasn't relief he felt. A man who loved her, who dreamed of marrying her would feel hurt, but she had done nothing to hurt him. In fact, she was the one apologizing as if she'd been at fault. If he loved her, he would feel hurt right now. She could hurt him. Hurt him as deeply as his mother had hurt him all these years. And if she hurt him, she would make him angry. As angry as he'd been with his mother. And he would hate her as he had hated—

He stopped the thoughts. Thoughts too treacherous to even be considered, too dangerous to be resolved rationally. He turned to Eden. "Yes, perhaps getting married would be a huge mistake." He watched her face, hoping for what? Some sign of protest, of disappointment? But for the first time her face was as unreadable as he knew his own to be.

She stood and smoothed her shirt. He stood to walk her out. At the door he saw her small smile and felt something shatter inside him.

"Eden."

It was those eyes that always undid him.

She reached up, touched his face. "Really, Brady, it's all right. Everything's all right."

Then she left. She was gone, and he just stood there. He hadn't made her angry or hurt her, but she'd left him all the same—just like his mother had left him years ago. Then, in an explosion of emotion, came the hurt, the anger, the hatred...and too late, the love.

SHE DIDN'T CRY as she came out of the lobby's artificial light into the mild spring evening. She wouldn't end this relationship in cliché. She'd told Brady everything was all right, and dammit, everything was going to be all right.

A few weeks ago, yes, she'd have been in tears by now. A few weeks ago she hadn't known the way a man's eyes darken with desire. She hadn't known what it was like to lie with a man, feel his touch, his taste, to fill yourself with him as if you were nothing but emptiness before. She hadn't known all these things, had only imagined them. She knew them now. Her imagination had been lacking.

Her eyes dry, her palms dry, even her mouth dry, she walked. A few weeks ago a man had never asked her to marry her. A few weeks ago she couldn't have imagined saying no.

It was twilight now. She walked on, feeling the solid span of her hips, the circle of her waist, the sound of her heels as they hit the walk. She passed her own building but didn't even look at it. Not yet. She continued on, learning the length of her arms, the strength in her legs, the press of her breasts. She walked until the sky went from gray to black and the air cooled, made her skin contract. In the past The Garden had always been her refuge, but she knew tonight she wouldn't find sanctuary there.

No, she wouldn't cry. Nor would she regret her relationship with Brady. It hadn't been love, but it had been something—something real and profound and wonderful. For the first time in her life, she'd realized desire, had been its source and its recipient. For that alone she was grateful.

And changed. She would never again be the woman she was before she'd been with Brady. She was better, stronger, more confident. She may never love anyone as much as she'd loved him nor in the same way, but her days of sitting around, too scared to find out were over.

Finally she turned toward home.

BRADY NODDED TO THE RESIDENT recently assigned to surgery. The resident held the door open, and they both passed into the corridor leading to the room assigned them.

"Nothing fancy today," Brady told the young man who'd be assisting him. "Routine gallbladder."

He entered the room just as the anesthetist was about to put his patient under. Prone on the table, the woman gave him a sidelong glance and smiled. Her hair capped, the sheet white across her, she looked even more vulnerable.

"All set, Mrs. Mattice?" He smiled as he took her wrist. His face would be the last thing she'd see before she closed her eyes in dreamless sleep. His eyes must be calm, his smile reassuring, his touch confident. He nodded to the anesthetist who pushed the plunger on the syringe attached to the IV tubing. The woman's breathing became regular. Her eyes closed. The circulating nurse uncovered and started to wash the belly.

Brady scrubbed in silence. The hands first, front and back, ten strokes minimum, then the fingers, the thin web of skin between them. There was an orange stick for scraping under the nails, then more scrubbing where the orange stick had been. The skin from the wrists to above the elbows was always the most tender. Then he rinsed off, resoaped his brush and started again, his skin turning pink, his thoughts focused, the Zen-like calm coming over him.

He backed through the door to the O.R., entering sideways, his arms raised, his hands held high as if offering alms. The room was all vague colors; the massive overhead lights, the metal of the instruments, the murmur of the machines all combining to create an abstract world. The scrub nurse handed him a sterile towel, opened a gown for him. The patient would be draped also, her face hidden, just as his own was masked.

He thrust his hands into the thin gloves, the routine familiar and flawless. "Prep," he said, noting his dry mouth, the tightening in the pit of his stomach. They were as familiar as the rest of the ritual, but, as he held his hands out for the final scrub solution, it was the sense of calm, control and strength that overtook all else now. As he approached the patient stretched out on the operating table, he remembered her words: *If I have to have any surgery done, I want you to do it, Dr. Spencer. I trust you.*

He took the clamped sponge, looked down at the shaved, white belly, felt the power in his purified hands. This woman had suffered. Today he would take away her pain.

It was only later when the incision had been made, the abdomen inflated, the scope inserted and he saw it—the surprising mass at the mouth of the bile duct that had somehow been hiding in the films—that he knew the woman had been wrong to place her trust in him. He had deceived her, failed her. He had no power.

"BRADY."

Someone was shaking him.

"Brady."

It'd been two days since Mrs. Mattice's operation. He'd taken out the gallbladder, most of the liver, cut away as much of the malignant tumor as possible and done a bile duct bypass. Not all of the tumor could be removed surgically. Too many blood vessels, too high a risk. There was chemo, radiation. Still the bottom line was Stage IV cancer. And Mrs. Mattice's face in his dreams.

He raised his head, blinking away the sleep, the dream images. He'd dreamed of Eden, too. He always dreamed of Eden.

"How long have you been here?"

His father loomed over the desk, staring down at him not unlike a dream caricature. Brady wondered if he'd woken up yet.

"All yesterday? All last night?" His father glanced at the dirty coffee cups on the desk.

Brady rubbed his face, ran his hands through his hair, tried to focus. Elias wasn't one for social calls. In fact, Brady couldn't remember him ever visiting his office.

"I went to your apartment building."

His father had never been to his condo, either. Elias expected people to come to him. Something was wrong.

"Is everything all right? Do you feel okay?"

"Don't worry. I'll be around a good many years yet to aggravate you and your brothers." Elias picked up one of the cups, glanced at the crumpled wrapper inside it. He threw the cup in the garbage with a disgusted snort. "Black coffee and cream cakes. Is that the FDA's most recent recommended dietary guidelines?"

Elias moved about the office, inspected the medical texts on the bookshelves, the binders of hospital policies, administrative memos. Brady knew he didn't come here to simply lecture. Something else had brought him here. He didn't bother asking him again. Whatever had brought his father here would be revealed when Elias was good and ready. Not a moment before.

Behind him Brady heard the sound of the blinds being opened. He waited.

"Weatherman said sunny and unseasonably warm, but I say rain from the look of those clouds and the cows lying in the fields. How long you plan on staying cooped up inside here?"

Brady straightened and felt the needles in his lower back from sleeping in a chair. "I have work to do." As soon as he said the words, he felt angry. He didn't have to explain his life, his choices. It was then he realized he was his father's son.

Elias circled the desk, settled in one of the wing chairs, the skepticism on his face telling Brady he wasn't buying any of it. Brady swallowed. There was a stale taste in his mouth. He wanted a hot shower and a steak. His hands scrubbed his face again, his skin feeling as wrinkled and as slack as he knew he looked.

He was brushing powdered sugar off the front of his Green Bay Packers T-shirt, wondering when he'd lost control, when his father said, "So, you and the girl, Eden...the marriage is off?"

Brady lifted his eyes back to his father. He wondered if his face was plaster-of-paris-white. "You know?"

His father smiled without humor. "Son, this is Tyler."

"And news travels fast."

"Bad news swifter than good."

The chair creaked as Brady swiveled toward the window. His father was right. It was going to rain.

"What happened?"

The question caught him like the flat of a hand against his face. Father-son talks weren't done in his family. Strong men didn't reveal themselves.

"We both agreed that it would be a mistake."

"Bull."

Brady turned, stared at his father. *What the hell did he want from him?*

"I saw the way that girl looked at you. And I saw the way you looked at her when you didn't think anyone was watching. What happened?"

"It was a misunderstanding."

Elias let out an exasperated breath. "That tells me diddly. Now, what happened?"

Brady looked at his father, hating the way he must look to him at that moment. He turned again toward the window. How could he explain when he himself wasn't sure what happened?

"She got some flowers. Roses."

"Another man?"

Brady nodded.

"Who? Not that ridiculous Flower Phantom the paper keeps wasting space on?"

Brady's lips curved but it wasn't a smile. "No."

"Humph." Elias huffed self-righteously. "Damn fool seems to send them to everybody else."

Everybody except the one person he should have sent them to, Brady thought. He turned back toward his father. "You're right. He is a damn fool."

"Does she love this other guy?" His father wasn't letting up.

Brady rested his forearms on the desk's polished surface, glad for the heavy width of wood, the solid, square boundary. He folded his hands. "You'd have to ask her that."

"I'm asking you."

"I can only give you an informed opinion."

Elias didn't even blink. "I didn't come here for you to give me jargon. I came here to find out what happened between you and this woman."

Brady's gaze was equally level. "I don't know if she loves him. I didn't ask her."

"Do you love her?"

"I don't know," he automatically responded.

His father studied him. "Yes, you do."

Yes, I do.

Elias stood as if to leave. Brady got up to walk him out, but his father didn't move toward the door.

"Your mother and I...our marriage was arranged." Elias looked past Brady to the window. "By our parents.

"The funny thing was I fell in love with her, your mother. I didn't plan on it. It just happened. That's the way it works."

Brady sank back into the chair. Elias stared out the window. His eyes saw the past. "You asked me once if I ever told her. Told her I loved her."

His gaze moved back to Brady. The faraway look left his eyes. "I didn't. Because I was too damned scared. Too damned scared she didn't love me. I don't know if she ever did or not. I never gave her the chance.

"She did love you boys, though. She contacted me soon after she left, begged me to let her see her sons. I told her I'd burn in hell before she ever set eyes on any of you again."

Brady said nothing. Too much emotion churned inside him. Elias was silent, too. They looked at each other, the years and years of silence between them.

Finally Elias broke the quiet. "Don't be a fool like your father, Brady."

Chapter Twelve

He went to The Garden. Past the display windows the lights were dim and there was no movement. He turned toward the alley when something in the front window caught his eye. There, propped between the lavender and pink flowers, the white and yellow buds, was one of Eden's paintings, its bold colors and strong lines made even more dramatic by the delicacy surrounding it.

Thatta girl, he thought. For the first time since Eden had broken the engagement, he smiled a genuine smile. As he stepped out from beneath the awning, he felt the first drops of rain.

The back door was also locked. She was out. With someone else? With Mr. Speedy Delivery?

As he turned he stumbled over something small and soft. He looked down. Penelope stared up at him, her expression irritated. She meowed, but in Brady's ears he heard her say, "Moron!"

"What are you doing out?" he asked the cat. "You have a hot date tonight too?"

Penelope licked one paw, then the other. She shot him a disdainful look and once more meowed. "Moron."

"Yeah, well, I'm not the one who chases my own tail."

In answer, the Persian stuck her bushy tail in the air, turned her backside to Brady and sauntered to the step. She circled once, settling into an elegant curve before sending him another insufferable look. Then, with a weary yawn, she shifted her gaze, dismissing him.

"If you're so smart, where's your mistress?"

Penelope continued to groom herself, ignoring him. The raindrops were falling faster now.

"What are you doing out here, anyway? I thought you were a house cat. Does Eden know you're out?"

Penelope granted him an insolent glance, then returned to licking her fur.

Brady stood in the rain, studying the animal. Sighing, he bent over and picked up the cat. He held her at arm's length, her body boneless, her expression disdainful. "Don't get any ideas. I'm only doing this for Eden." He could've sworn the cat smirked. "C'mon, let's go find her and bring her home."

JENNA BALLED UP the wrapping paper and handed it to Molly who was holding a large green garbage bag. Jenna removed the top off the box, pulling back the tissue paper. She smiled as she lifted a doll-size sweater from the box. "Look." She pointed to the

Winnie the Pooh at the sweater's border, eliciting a chorus of oohs and aahs. She held up the hat and booties, each with their own embroidered miniature Poohs. The chorus sounded again.

Eden balanced a paper plate of vegetables and dip on her lap as she passed two layette sets to Tisha on her right. Nadine on her left handed her a diaper bag filled with rattles, bottles, undershirts, teething toys. In the front of the room, Jenna neatly folded the sweater back into the box, her hand resting lovingly on it a second before she gave it to Molly to add to the growing pile of presents waiting to make the rounds of the gathered guests. Molly returned with a much larger gift-wrapped box.

"Ladies, there's fresh punch," Anna called from the doorway. Originally the party was to be held out in the Breakfast Inn Bed's landscaped back lawn, but the rain had forced the affair to be quickly moved inside. The food and drink had been set up on the tables in the inn's dining room. Here, in the living room, the Victorian-style sofas and chairs had been pushed against the walls to make room for the rows of folding chairs. The sounds of conversation and laughter drifted in from the hall as guests got up to refill their plate or cup and lingered in the foyer. Some of the husbands had come, too, and were up in Molly and Quinn's apartment on the third floor, playing cards. Only a few minutes ago Quinn and Seth, en route to raiding the food tables again for the men upstairs, had come to the doorway and said hello. Their deeper voices now mingled with the others in the hall and dining room.

Eden fingered the soft cotton of a sleeper, touched the yellow satin bow at its neckline. She lifted the cotton booties out of the box, placing them in the flat of her palm.

Tisha picked up one of the booties. "So small, they hardly seem real, do they?"

Eden smiled. "No." She passed the sleeper set, retrieved her paper cup of punch from where she'd set it on the floor beneath her chair.

This is how it's done, she thought. *Someone speaks and you answer. Someone smiles and you smile back. Lift a cup to your mouth. Sip. Swallow. Put the cup back beneath the chair where it won't get spilled, take the gift from Nadine.* There, she'd gotten through fifteen more seconds. Fifteen more seconds of being without Brady.

Jenna had to stand the large present on one end to unwrap it. Now with Molly helping to hold the oversize box, she took the top off. From inside, Jenna lifted a corner of colorful cloth. She pulled until a long rectangle of color and pattern and print settled across the swollen curve of her belly as if already warming the children inside her. Appreciative murmurs and more oohs and aahs came from the crowd, but Jenna was silent as she stared at the handcrafted quilt. She touched the blanket's tiny, hand-sewn stitches, the carefully appliquéd cow jumping over a crescent moon, the pastel cat playing a fiddle. She lifted her gaze, tilting her head back as if afraid the tears that had begun would stain the beautifully crafted symbol of love, and caring spread across her.

Tisha rummaged in her purse. "Those lovely ladies," she murmured, her own eyes glossy. She pulled out a tissue and carefully wiped beneath her lower lashes so as not to smear her mascara. "They're working on a new quilt, you know. A wedding design."

"That's nice. For whom?" Eden made small talk.

Tisha shrugged as she blew her nose. "You know the Quilting Circle. They never say. But they always know."

Several guests had gotten up to inspect the quilt closer. They gathered around Jenna, the blanket still displayed across her belly, and admired the quality of workmanship, the blending of color and cloth. From her seat, Eden admired the blanket, also, seeing many of the same quiet pastels that currently colored her shop windows. Soothing shades now joined by the soulful hues of her own paintings. Her paintings, so long buried, now bravely, brazenly, exposed for the world to see. Yesterday one of Jenna's old colleagues, a gallery owner from New York City, who'd come to town for the baby shower, had seen the paintings and come into the shop, asking who the artist was.

Artist. Imagine, Eden thought.

The gallery owner, Sue, had then asked if there were any more paintings she could look at, said she saw a soul released in the work.

A soul released. Imagine.

While Christy watched the store, Eden had brought Sue upstairs and shown her the rest of her work. Afterward, they'd exchanged business cards, and Sue said she'd be in touch. Eden didn't expect anything to come of it. It had been exciting enough to have her art admired by someone from the New York City art world.

A soul released...

That was her thought, colored in the rich patina of her paintings, when the rustling and murmurs of the guests seemed to swell. Eden saw Jenna look up from the quilt.

The knot of women gathered around Jenna raised their heads, as well, their gazes going to the doorway. Several women in front of Eden shifted in their chairs, turning their heads toward the back. She was about to glance over her shoulder to see what had caught the others' attention when she heard without preamble or apology, "I'm looking for Eden."

Brady. The colors in her head seemed to burst inside her.

She turned her head and stared. She couldn't speak.

He stood in the doorway, his gaze moving about the confusion of bows and balloons, pastel-colored swags, cradles filled with gifts, crowns of women's hair, sprayed, fluffed, teased and curled.

"Eden?"

She wasn't sure she could stand. She wasn't sure she could breath. His gaze searched the room. He wore jeans faded to white and an untucked, wrinkled T-shirt, its wet material clinging to his body, outlining the tense muscle of his torso. His hair was wet, too, and uncombed. Yet even in its damp state, several cowlicks stuck up above the limp strands. His face was dark with a day's beard, and there were two long scratches down one cheek, both a bright, fresh red.

He ran his hands through his hair, adding fresh disarray while his eyes kept searching. She could see Seth and Quinn behind him. Stares shifted toward her now.

"Brady?"

His gaze darted in the direction of her voice.

She slowly rose and holding on to the back of her chair, she faced him.

He looked at her, then came toward her, the urgency never leaving his eyes. The women slid their chairs aside, cutting him a path.

He stopped several feet away from her. "I brought Penelope."

She saw her cat in Quinn's arms. She nodded. She didn't know what to say. She traced her cheek with a fingertip, silently noting his scratches.

He touched his cheek, surprise in his eyes when he felt the scratches, as if unaware of them before. "She was outside. It was raining. I was afraid..." He stopped, looked into her eyes. She'd never heard his voice tremble before. "I was afraid."

He glanced around the room as if only now realizing there were others surrounding them, their gazes curious.

His gaze shifted to the far wall where there were no eyes. "Those flowers. Those roses." He brought his gaze back to her, a mixture of emotions in his eyes. Sadness. Regret. Anger. Pain. "I should have sent them. Those roses. They should've been from me."

Eden told herself she wasn't going to cry. She felt the prickling behind her lids and pressed her teeth together so she wouldn't blink. She wouldn't cry. She shook her head, telling him no, it wasn't his fault.

"Yes." The command had returned to his voice. "Yes," she heard again, softer. She looked at him, saw the tenderness in those turbulent green eyes.

"I wish I had sent them."

He ran his fingers through his hair, exhaling a heavy breath. "I've held a human heart in my hand, massaged it until it came back to life, but I've no idea how it works. I've seen a skull sectioned, can name you every part and function of the human brain, but I can't explain why we behave the way we do. I don't know why I started sending flowers secretly, sometimes to complete strangers."

She heard soft gasps, saw the surprised expressions. Seth was looking at Quinn, astonished. Brady seemed oblivious to the response caused by his revelation.

"I know it was easier. Easier than reaching out to someone right in front of me, easier than saying,

'Don't go. Don't leave me.'" His hands came up, hung helplessly.

"I let you go, and I don't know why. I held the door for you and let you walk right out of my life when all I wanted was to grab you and hang on for dear life."

His hands reached toward her. Her tears came.

"Because that's what you are to me—life. That I do know. I thought I knew so much more. And if others think I know so much more, I let them think it. But I don't know anything anymore. I don't know anything...but you. There's nothing else."

He looked past her, his gaze unseeing. "We all know pain. A doctor fights it. A man rages against it. But a woman...a woman...she reaches out her hand, and there's healing."

Eden heard the sound of others' tears. She saw only Brady before her. His gaze met hers.

"It will take time with me, but I'm changing. You changed me."

She shook her head.

He took a step. "Don't leave me, Eden. Stay with me. Stay with me."

He took another step, looking at her with those green, green eyes, and she felt extraordinary, more than mere flesh and bone, but spectacular as if her skin were the sky and her spirit the heat of the sun. Yet, even then, made wondrous as Heaven above, she waited, wanting, needing one more thing from this man.

"I love you, Eden."

She heard the words she'd been waiting to hear forever and became beautiful all over.

Finally she spoke. "I love you, Brady."

"Marry me?"

"Yes," she said as he came to her. "Yes, yes, yes," she said as he gathered her in his arms and the room rang with applause.

Then she said nothing as his mouth found hers, and they clung to each other, mouth to mouth, body to body, holding tightly to what had almost been taken from them. She twined her arms around his unshaven neck, tasting this man and her own tears.

The kiss ended, but her arms still circled his neck, keeping him close enough to feel his breath against her cheek. He kissed away a tear. She looked into the green of his eyes.

"Take me home," she asked. "To The Garden. Take me home and make love to me."

There were a few gasps but many more sighs and smiles as Brady picked her up in his arms and carried her out of the room, past Quinn still holding Penelope, past Seth smiling, and out the front door.

He looked down at her when they reached the walk. "Your reputation is beyond ruin now."

She tipped her head back, laughter spilling out as happiness filled her. "Finally. And now you're going to go and spoil it all by making a decent woman of me."

He pressed her tight to his chest. "We've given the town of Tyler enough to talk about."

She looked up, seeing her future in the face

above. She saw a long, happy life with children and family and flowers. Most of all, she saw the man she loved now and always. "Yes," she said softly, "and that was some grand finale you just put on in there."

"That wasn't the finale." He smiled at her. "Not by a long shot."

EDEN LOOKED DOWN at the bouquet she'd crafted— duchess rosebuds, clusters of rose petals, ivy, beads, silk streamers. She looked over her shoulder to see if the others were ready. Some had come eagerly; others had to be prodded. The group was getting smaller at each subsequent wedding. She saw Christy at the front, on the edge of womanhood, and Martha Bauer by her side, playfully elbowing her over. Coming to the group was Marge. The diner owner had sprained her ankle and had needed help getting around so she'd brought Caroline Benning to the wedding as her guest. However, it was Marge who was dragging Caroline to the floor. The tall, pretty blonde stood to the side of the circle, her arms wrapped around her waist, looking uneasy.

"Wait for me." Waving a taloned hand, Nadine ran over from where she'd been talking to the band, the long satin skirt of her bridesmaid dress gathered in her hand. Lydia squeezed over, making room for her within the knot of women. Eden looked at them and saw so many special friends. She looked around, seeing many more friends and family—her parents up from Florida, looking tanned and healthy, Molly and Jenna in their pale satin gowns, Quinn and Seth in dark tuxes, Sara spinning, enjoying the swish of her first long skirt. There was Gina, not much more than a new bride herself, Jeff and Cece Baron holding hands, Tisha smoothing stray strands of hair off Judson's forehead. Everywhere she looked, Eden saw love and happiness.

She found Brady, looking strong and handsome in his black tuxedo. He was laughing with a colleague, the lines of his face no longer tight but full with joy. As if sensing her gaze, he looked over at her and smiled.

"Are we ready?" the lead singer asked into the microphone. Eden tore her gaze away from Brady, gave a final glance at the women gathered behind her, then turned her back to them as the band struck up a tune. The lead singer counted, "One. Two. Three." Eden lobbed the bouquet over her head, hearing the shouts of the women. She turned as the cluster was breaking apart and saw Lydia raising the flowers triumphantly as she looked over at Elias and winked. The smile left Elias's face.

A chair was carried to the center of the dance area and Eden sat as Brady was pushed forward. The band broke into a sultry tune. Brady gave her a suggestive smile. His hips swiveled as he moved slowly toward her. When he undid his tie and threw it to the crowd, the women cheered and Eden tipped her head back and laughed. He unbuttoned his shirt collar, dancing seductively toward her as if it were natural to see Dr. Brady Spencer bump and grind in front of the entire town.

He reached her and bent down on one knee, his hands finding her offered ankle. She smiled at him. "You realize you've now become as silly as the rest of the human race?"

He stroked her calf, sending currents of desire through her. "It's about time, don't you think?"

She pulled the satin skirt up a few more inches. His hands lingered on her knee, his fingers circling it slowly. He leaned forward, kissing its knobby rise. Eden heard the catcalls and scattered applause.

He looked up at her, his emerald eyes loving her. "You're blushing."

She hiked the skirt one more inch above her knee. His hands slid beneath her skirt, traced a line where the garter lace met her thigh. Slowly he drew the garter down, his fingertips trailing across the inside of her thigh, brushing the soft spot behind her knee, skimming the curve of her calf until the lacy garter circled her ankle.

"Can you make sure your father gets that?" she asked him as he slid the lace circle off her foot.

He smiled. "It's being arranged as we speak." He stood, victorious, spinning the garter on one finger as the guests clapped and cheered. He looked at Eden, then leaned over and kissed her. He looked into her eyes, his own suddenly sober. "I never thought I'd love anyone this much."

She laid her hand against his cheek. "I never thought anyone would love me this much."

"That's the easy part."

"I love you, Brady."

"I love you." He lightly kissed her once more and giving her his hand, helped her up. She took her place on the sidelines as the lead singer instructed the single men to go to the middle.

Stretching the garter, Brady looked at the men gathering. "There's not many of you guys left, is there, fellas? Come on, Coop, don't be chicken. Come up a little farther toward the front." He met his friend's dark scowl and laughed.

As the band began to play, Brady turned, waited for the count, then threw the slip of elastic and lace back into the crowd.

He saw the others step back, leaving his father alone as the garter dropped directly in front of him. Brady looked at Eden and winked. "Bull's-eye," he mouthed.

The sun was setting by the time the last guest left. Molly joined Jenna and Eden still sitting at one of the linen-covered tables arranged around the lawn. "Sara's sleeping on the daybed," she said as she pulled out a chair. "I never expected her to make it this long without her afternoon nap."

"It was all the excitement," Jenna said.

"She was a terrific flower girl," Eden told Molly.

"It was a terrific wedding."

Eden looked around at the latticed pavilion decorated with tulle, roses and ivy, the flower-filled stone urns, the arched trellis that had turned the grounds of the Spencer family home into an open wedding garden. Elias himself had insisted on clearing the old beds himself and planting the rows and rows of primroses and impatiens, geraniums and petunias. "Yes, it was wonderful."

Jenna pulled out another chair and propped her feet on it. "Look at those ankles." She looked down at the puffy, shiny flesh poking out from the hem of her bridesmaid's gown. She laughed. "Well, I always did think my legs were too skinny."

"And it won't be long now." Molly smiled at her.

Jenna patted the curve of her belly. "I know." She looked at Eden. "What about you and Brady? Are you going to have children right away?"

"Wait a minute." Brady, who'd been standing nearby with his brothers and Coop, came over to the table and pulled out the chair next to Eden. "Don't we at least get a honeymoon first?"

"You'll have to excuse my wife," Seth said as he joined them, "but I'm sure you can understand why the only thing she thinks about these days is babies." He leaned over and kissed Jenna's forehead. She patted his cheek.

The back screen door opened as Elias came outside and headed toward the group.

"Here comes Grandpa now," Seth said.

"He looks a little pale." Brady noted.

"He's hasn't recovered since Lydia caught the bouquet," Quinn said.

Elias smiled as he reached the others, but his expression remained pensive. "Are you okay, Dad?" Brady asked.

"I'm fine." Still he seemed troubled.

"It seems like something is bothering you," Brady persisted.

Elias waved his hand. "It's nothing."

"What's nothing?"

He looked at Brady, the others at the table. "Something happened earlier. Really it's nothing." Still the others looked at him, waiting expectantly. He sighed. "All right. This afternoon when the cake was being served, I went inside. I wanted to get an antacid."

"I guess Sara wasn't the only one who had too much excitement today."

"You don't feel well, Dad?" Brady got up.

"No, that's not it. I'm fine. I'm fine. Really." Elias gestured for his son to sit down. "It's just when I went in, that blonde, the new girl that came to town a few months ago—"

"Caroline Benning?" Coop supplied, his eyes narrowing.

"Yes, Caroline, that's right. She was inside the house, too. In my office."

"In your office?" Seth looked at his father. "What was she doing in there?"

"She had taken a picture off my desk. A family picture. She was looking at it."

"What picture? I don't remember any pictures on your desk." Quinn looked at his brothers.

"This is an old picture. Taken only a few weeks

before your mother left. It's been in my desk drawer all these years. You boys have never seen it. I never put it out…until today.''

He looked at his family. ''It seemed like it was time.'' He paused. ''Anyway, when I went into the house, there was Caroline holding the picture, studying it.''

Cooper looked at the others. ''First she's found tangled up in the shrubs, now she's snooping around inside the house.''

''Do you think she was just curious about the picture? Maybe she was seeing how we've changed since we were kids,'' Brady suggested.

''Could be,'' Elias considered. His expression stayed thoughtful. ''You know, there's something about that girl… I can't quite put my finger on it. It's probably just my imagination…'' His voice trailed off.

''What is it?'' Brady asked.

Elias again made a dismissive gesture. ''It's just that every time I look at that old family photo, it strikes me again.'' He looked to the fields beyond. ''It's nothing really. It's just that sometimes, that girl, Caroline, she tilts her head or the light hits her just so or once when I saw her smile today…then I see it.''

Elias's sons looked at each other, then back at their father. ''See what?''

''The resemblance.'' Elias looked at all of them. ''I look at Caroline, and I see your mother.''

LATE THAT NIGHT, Eden turned in the darkness to her new husband beside her. "Do you think your father is all right?" They were leaving for Europe tomorrow, but they'd chosen to stay in Eden's apartment tonight. Brady had already put his condo on the market. Today Molly had mentioned a restored Victorian with a huge garden on Ivy Street had just gone on the market. "What do you think he was trying to say today with all that business about Caroline and your mother?"

Brady pulled her closer, breathed in her scent. "I'm not sure. I don't know if he was sure what he was trying to say." He yawned contentedly, Eden warm in his arms and all worries seeming far outside these bedroom walls. "I do know one thing. If Caroline Benning is up to something, she might better leave town now. Because Coop won't be leaving that lady alone until he has found out everything there is to find out about that woman and what she's doing in Tyler. I almost feel sorry for the girl."

"Yes, Coop did have that Joe Friday look when he left," Eden murmured, nestled against Brady's shoulder. "The Flower Phantom wouldn't have survived a week if Coop had been put on the case."

Brady was silent, thinking of today and the days before, the many years without Eden and the last few months with her. He thought of how he almost let her go, how they almost lost each other, both too scared to believe in love. He smoothed the soft curls from her brow. "Happy?" he whispered. Her even breaths answered him, and he heard the rattle of sleep as she sighed. He brushed his lips against her forehead, then, not yet ready to end this day, he slid out of the bed, careful not to wake her. He sat in the rocking chair. The same chair where he'd sat, watching Eden sleep, after they'd made love for the first time. His eyes adjusted to the darkness. He saw once again the canopy bed, the vines of silk flowers twined around its frame. He saw Eden, the delicate shapes of her face outlined against the white linen, her soft breaths ruffling the edge of the pillowcase. He resisted the urge to slip back between the covers and curl up beside her, wanting to prolong the day, the sweet, simple joy of watching a woman sleep.

She shifted. The quilt covering her gently rippled, its embroidered flowers seeming to sway. It had been a wedding present from the Quilting Circle. They'd said its pattern was called The Unexpected Garden. Martha Bauer, they'd confided, had picked it out several weeks ago and made them start drafting the pieces right away. It was later when Eden had been unfolding the blanket across the bed that they discovered the words embroidered in small, even stitches across the spread's ivory backing:

"Now the Lord God had planted a garden in the east, in Eden; and there he put the man he had formed. Genesis 2:8."

Something brushed against Brady's bare legs. Penelope bounded into his lap and settled herself across his thighs. Her pupils wide, she gazed up at him as if trying to decide if she should tolerate him.

He leaned down, whispering, "I know you really

like me,'' and kissed her longhaired crown. Penelope turned her head, refusing to look at him, but her body relaxed and became long and heavy across his lap as he scratched her behind the ears.

The night was quiet, as were all Tyler nights. Brady soundlessly rocked, his hand stroking Penelope's long back. Eden shifted once more, burrowing beneath the quilt. Penelope stretched, purred. Brady rocked and watched the woman who'd brought him love, life. The minutes went by and the night waned. Still Brady sat, happy as a man could be, here with Eden…his unexpected garden.

* * * * *

RETURN TO TYLER

continues next month with

BRIDE OF DREAMS

by Linda Randall Wisdom.

Don't miss this exciting story, available in March, from Harlequin American Romance.

From bestselling
Harlequin American Romance author

CATHY GILLEN THACKER

comes

TEXAS VOWS

A McCABE FAMILY SAGA

Sam McCabe had vowed to always
do right by his five boys—but after
the loss of his wife, he needed the small-town security
of his hometown, Laramie, Texas, to live up to that
commitment. Except, coming home would bring him
back to a woman he'd sworn to stay away from.
It will be one vow that Sam can't keep....

On sale March 2001

Available at your favorite retail outlet.

HARLEQUIN®
Makes any time special ™

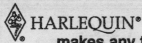

HARLEQUIN®
makes any time special—online...

eHARLEQUIN.com

your romantic
books

♥ **Shop online!** Visit Shop eHarlequin and discover a wide selection of new releases and classic favorites at great discounted prices.

♥ **Read** our daily and weekly Internet exclusive serials, and participate in our interactive novel in the reading room.

♥ **Ever dreamed of being a writer?** Enter your chapter for a chance to become a featured author in our Writing Round Robin novel.

your romantic
life

♥ **Check out** our feature articles on dating, flirting and other important romance topics and get your daily love dose with tips on how to keep the romance alive every day.

your
community

♥ **Have** a Heart-to-Heart with other members about the latest books and meet your favorite authors.

♥ **Discuss** your romantic dilemma in the Tales from the Heart message board.

your romantic
escapes

♥ **Learn** what the stars have in store for you with our daily Passionscopes and weekly Erotiscopes.

♥ **Get** the latest scoop on your favorite royals in Royal Romance.

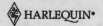

HARLEQUIN®

AMERICAN *Romance*

This small Wisconsin town
has some big secrets...and the
newest scandal is about to hit!

**RETURN
TO
TYLER**

SECRET BABY SPENCER
by Jule McBride
11/00 AR #849

**PRESCRIPTION FOR
SEDUCTION**
by Darlene Scalera
2/01 AR #861

PATCHWORK FAMILY
by Judy Christenberry
12/00 AR #853

BRIDE OF DREAMS
by Linda Randall Wisdom
3/01 AR #865

And in January 2001, be sure to look for this special
3-in-1 collection from Harlequin Books!

TYLER BRIDES
by Kristine Rolofson
Heather MacAllister
Jacqueline Diamond

*Warm as a cherished family quilt and bright
as a rainbow, these stories weave together
the fabric of a community.*

Available at your favorite retail outlet.

HARLEQUIN®
Makes any time special ™

Visit us at www.eHarlequin.com

HARRTT

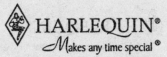

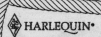
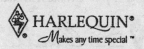

#1 *New York Times* bestselling author

NORA ROBERTS

brings you more of the loyal and loving,
tempestuous and tantalizing Stanislaski family.

Coming in February 2001

The Stanislaski Sisters

Natasha and Rachel

Though raised in the Old World traditions of their
family, fiery Natasha Stanislaski and cool, classy
Rachel Stanislaski are ready for a *new* world of love....

*And also available in February 2001 from
Silhouette Special Edition, the newest book in the
heartwarming Stanislaski saga*

CONSIDERING KATE

Natasha and Spencer Kimball's daughter Kate turns her
back on old dreams and returns to her hometown, where
she finds the *man* of her dreams.

Available at your favorite retail outlet.

Where love comes alive™